transpose

transpose
a self-styled revolution

Matt Padwick

Published by Inner Temple Press
Castletownbere, West Cork, Ireland

inner.temple.press@gmail.com

See also
www.mattpadwick.com

ISBN: 978-0-9931840-3-1

Also by Matt Padwick
Running Contra Diction (2015)

transpose

1. To change to the opposite position, direction, or course.
2. To change or alter into a different form, nature, substance, or state.

trans-

A prefix meaning across or through, used in particular to form verbs denoting movement or conveyance from place to place (transfer; transmit; transplant) or complete change (transform; transmute).
Or to form adjectives meaning crossing, on the other side of or going beyond the place named.

pose

1. To set forth in words for consideration; propound, pose a question.
2. To assume or hold a particular position or posture.
3. To represent oneself falsely; pretend to be other than what one is. (A studied or artificial manner or attitude, often assumed in an attempt to impress or deceive others.)

Kendo saying:
When you focus on losing, you will lose.
When you focus on winning, you will lose.
Pay attention to your inner balance,
then perhaps you have a chance to win.

outward

heavy

The car lurched forward and stalled on a patch of bare earth under the shade of a tree outside a prefabricated house in the Florida swamplands. The driver's door opened and a body fell out. Then the passenger's door opened, a second body hit the ground with a thud. There was no sign of blood, just the creaking and cranking noises when very hot metal starts to cool down.

A dark-haired man and a blond woman were standing on the porch of the house. He walked towards the car. She went back into the house to get a jug of water.

"The disadvantage…with this car is…" said the red-faced driver between gulps of cold water, "…is the engine overheats…and the only way to stop it…overheating…is to have the heater on full…which cools the engine down but heats up the car…a lot."

Outside it was humid and thirty degrees. Inside the car, which was a 1971 Chevrolet Chevelle Malibu Sport Sedan, it had been nearly treble that.

A few minutes later the driver had recovered enough to stand up and make some introductions.

"Hi, Jake. It's Ed. And this is Tracy."

Jake looked blankly at the couple who had just arrived.

The driver tried again. "Jake?"

"Yes."

"Do you remember me now?"

"No."

"I'm Ed. From the Bahamas. You said to drop by if I ever came to Florida."

"Oh, Ed. The Bahamas. Yeah. How are you? And Tracy was it?

"Yep, that's right. Ed – and Tracy."

"Okay. Tracy and Ed. Hi. Yeah. Pleased to meet you."

The blond woman was glaring at Jake. Jake got the message.

"Oh yeah. This is my…this is Jayne."

Jake and Jayne's relationship was on the rocks. They spoke to their guests, but they didn't speak to each other.

While Jake was outside faking busyness Ed and Tracy were sitting at the kitchen table watching Jayne pop ice-cubes into a jug of Tang. Tracy was dressed in a fresh *Metallica* vest, with a combed mohican and freshly plaited goatee beard. Ed had tied his dreadlocks back, he was wearing his best shorts and one of Jake's t-shirts – just until the washing was done.

Jayne had already decided the visitors were decent people, polite and with a sense of humour – quite different from the man she had married – and had asked them if they wanted to go into town for a meal and some wine.

"Eh, sorry, we can't, we're going for a beer with Jake's softball team."

"Ah well," she said, "good luck with that. The bars round here are full of toothless folk covered in tattoos…Oh, I mean ugly tattoos, not body art."

Tracy held up a hand as if to say *no offence taken.* Jayne had already paid compliment to the celtic designs covering his arms and legs, and admired most of his many piercings.

There was nothing soft about Jake's softball team. Despite being thrown off the league two seasons ago they still met up for practice at Ronnie's Bar two evenings a week, which was in preparation for "match days" which lasted for most of most weekends. Jake was the last of them to get his divorce through.

That was all on a Sunday.

On Monday morning the boys had tropical hang-overs. Jake scraped them up and drove them to The Old Ponderosa Fish Camp. It was like a movie set; feathery vines hung from the cypress trees accentuating the stony silence. Jake wanted Tracy to help design and build a new jetty while Ed was teamed up with Ronald to demolish and remove the old toilet block.

Ronald was an ex-marine, a veteran of every conflict for which his country deemed him eligible, a career that had spanned the golden age of American warmongery. And when he retired from the marines he became a mercenary. Now he was properly retired. Helping Jake break things was just a hobby.

Ronald had *sweet* inked under one of his nipples and *sour* under the other. He told Ed that. Ed would never have dared to read it for himself.

Demolishing the toilet block was easy. Ronald reversed the truck into one wall and it collapsed like a pack of cards. Unfortunately Ed was inside the building doing a recce at the time. Fortunately he had been standing by a window, the glass long-gone, so when the walls collapsed inwards he jumped out of the window. He was unhurt but a little shaken, not too shaken to hide though.

Ronald circled the rubble calling for Ed a few times before shrugging his shoulders and setting off to tell Jake his new assistant had been killed in the line of duty. Which is when Ed came out from behind a tree.

"Hey, Ronald, just taking a leak, now, what's next?"

"Load this here truck," said Ronald neither pleased nor relieved.

Each time the truck was full of debris Ronald drove them to the dump, hunched over the steering wheel and chain-smoking as they rumbled down the narrow tarmac alleyways that divided the swamp.

At lunchtime they went to the gas station at Molasses Junction for a filled roll and a can of coke. The proprietor was sitting on a rocking chair, knitting. She finished the row and set down her pipe before getting up to serve them.

At the end of the day on the way home, they nearly crashed into a crop-spraying bi-plane that was banking into a turn to start a new row. "That fuckin Frankie has inhaled too much DDT…"

Pulling up at Jake's place Ronald spotted the car parked on the bare earth under the tree. "It's a 350 V8, that dual exhaust would give it two hundred horsepower. We call 'em the Heavy Chevy, " he said.

"It's a micro-wave bloody oven that's what it is!" said Ed. Just looking at it made him sweat. Instinctively his face went into *the driving frown* which had helped stop the perspiration running off his forehead and stinging his eyes. Ed explained the overheating issue to Ronald.

"Ronald, do you know anyone who wants to buy a Chevy-shaped micro-wave oven?"

"Mmmm. You might get something for it in winter. In Canada."

"We're not driving it to Canada. We're scared of it. It's like being in hell already…"

Ronald walked round the car, sizing it up.

"What the fuck kind of license plate is that anyway man?"

"It's a *temporary tag*. It was part of the deal." Ed explained how they'd been talking with the car salesmen when a uniformed debt collector showed up, ushered the salesman into the sales office and berated him for ten minutes.

This had given Ed and Tracy time to think. The Heavy Chevy was already the cheapest car on the lot, but it was more than they could afford. And a license plate would cost more than the car.

When the salesman emerged looking a foot shorter Ed faked disinterest while Tracy pushed for half price – but including a temporary license tag written out till the end of the month, which would give them a thirty-day grace period to find the money for a real license plate.

Then Ed entered the negotiation saying he would only agree if they also received two more thirty day tags – blank ones – which they could fill in and slap on as needed. The car was sick, with a life-expectancy of much less than ninety days, but it would be a handy insurance to have just in case. Of course this was all against the law but the beleaguered salesman had to agree; he needed cash.

Ronald liked the story. "You guys are illeegaal!" he said exposing all of his gums. Suddenly they were family. "I'll take a look at this car for you. *If* you send me a post-card from Canada."

"Uh? No way! We're not even going to Canada, that was your idea."

"Have we got a deal or is this fucked up car of yours going to rot under this here tree?"

Jake had already warned Ed and Tracy that there was no god-damn way that this illeeegal wreck of a god-damn car was going to rot under his god-damn tree.

Ed had to think quickly. He couldn't.

"It's a deal. A postcard from Canada it is."

Jake was an alcoholic. Jayne was taking night classes to better herself. That, in a nutshell, was their problem.

On Friday lunchtime Jake went missing. On Friday night Jayne took Ed and Tracy to a comedy club in the city. In the bar afterwards they met the evening's best comedian. He bit his finger nails continuously and wasn't funny at all. They got back really late. Jayne looked at Tracy a moment longer than was necessary before announcing she was going to bed. It was Ed's turn on the couch but Tracy got there first so Ed laid himself out on the floor. The house was quiet for a few minutes. Then Jake arrived home and somehow pulled the fridge down on top

of himself while putting milk on his cornflakes.
On Saturday night all four of them sat on the long sofa. Jake was at one end, Jayne was at the other, the lads were in the middle. The beer was warm because the fridge was broken.

TV was mostly ads. Jayne was staring at a magazine until something worth watching came on.

Jake got Tracy to help him bring out a second TV from the bedroom, they put it next to the first one, wired up his Playstation and loaded the *Formula 1* game. So on the left screen they had advertisements blaring and flashing at them, broken up by chat shows and soaps. And on the right screen they had Formula 1 with the settings on really hard so only Tracy and Jake could cope with it. Tracy had spent years on a sofa learning to cope in front of his Playstation. Jake had obviously wasted a lot of time getting really good at it too.

Inspired by a TV news item, Ed attempted conversation.

"America is crazy," he said. "I don't mean crazy, I mean, y'know, *mad*. You can't drink alcohol in public but anyone can own an automatic weapon."

"Some people can do more damage drinking," said Jayne.

Oh. They went back to silence.

That was Saturday night. On Sunday morning Jake announced he was going to Bobby the Dinosaur's fiftieth birthday party. He looked at Ed and Tracy. Jayne was looking at Ed and Tracy. Ed and Tracy looked at the floor. They knew this was a test – one they could never pass.

Out on the road a car horn sounded. Everyone looked at Jake. Nothing he said now could make any difference. He said nothing. He closed the door behind himself and skipped off down the dusty path to play with his friends.

At five that afternoon there was a phone call. Jayne picked it up and listened for thirty seconds while her head inflated and reddened, then she slammed the handset down without having said a word.

She disappeared into the bedroom and crashed around for half a minute before emerging with a small suitcase.

"I'm sorry you had to see this. I'm leaving. Goodbye."

The little house shook as she slammed the door. Ed spilled his can of warm beer. Tracy was winning the Australian Grand Prix at the Adelaide Street Circuit but the commotion had punctured his concentration; he hit a barrier on the Dequetteville Hairpin, losing his front wing.

"Shit! What just happened?" he said twitching on the sofa (lowering a shoulder as he took each bend and flicking his right foot when he changed gear).

A minute later the phone rang again. Tracy crashed again. "Shiiiit!"

He threw the console to the ground. His race was over.

Ed picked up the telephone handset and nervously put it to his ear. The caller sounded a bit like Jake. It was Jake. What was left of him. He was on a pay-phone, he needed to be collected from Papa Joe's Bar. He started giving directions while Ed was looking for a pen. Ed got some of it down but then Jake must have run out of change and the phone cut off.

Ed and Tracy drove Jake's pick-up deep into the swamp-jungle looking for Papa Joe's. All the cross-roads looked the same – they went straight over some, turned left at others, sometimes they turned right, until they gave up looking for the bar and decided their goal was to make it out of there while there was still gas in the tank. Which is when they found Papa Joe's.

As they walked towards the shack the night-time jungle noises were overtaken by the sound of a jukebox. On the porch an empty rocking-chair was gently rocking. There was a sprinkling of blood on the wooden step. The door was wedged open with a flattened Budweiser can.

Ed was unshaven, had dreadlocks and was wearing board shorts. He looked like most of the other women in there.

Tracy had Celtic tattoos, face and body-piercing, a mohican, goatee and a sunburned neck. There was a triangle of "females" buzzing around him in seconds.

"Woo wee, ain't he pretty," said the first.

"Ooh, there's one hell of an accent you got there," said the second who was six-feet-two not including her floppy straw hat. She flashed her gums at Tracy. "You know how to handle yourself, don't you boy?"

Jake was nowhere to be seen.

There was a sign over the bar saying Tequila Sam's.

A slow song came on. The ladies started fighting over who was going to dance with Tracy while their mothers were focussed on Ed.

Ed and Tracy got home a little before daybreak. Jake was asleep next to the Heavy Chevy on the patch of bare earth under the tree outside his prefabricated house.

You know things are serious when there is no humour.

At lunchtime Jake and Ed and Tracy congregated in the kitchen around a cereal box, taking a handful and passing it on. Ed looked up from a *Reader's Digest* magazine. "You know that famous conundrum, *If a tree falls in the forest and no one is there, does it still make a sound?...*"

"For Christ's sake, Scrambles, pack it in. Have you no respect for a decent hangover! Sorry Jake, he does this sometimes. Often in fact."

"I don't get it," said Jake. Poor Jake. The story of how the lads escaped from Tequila Sam's had momentarily cheered him but now, again, he looked like a fallen tree, broken and alone in the forest of his fucked up life.

"Well," said Tracy, "what he said, said in a different way is, if a man speaks and there isn't a woman there to hear him, is he still wrong?"

"Ah, it's a tongue twister, I get it."

In the afternoon of that day Jake phoned Jayne at her mother's place. Jayne asked him why he wasn't working. Jake said he wasn't at work because he had a headache and a fever, because yesterday, at the party, he'd been bitten by a spider.

hitched

His name was Ed. His nickname was Scrambled Ed. On leaving school he had taken a year out to decide what he wanted to study at university. The year passed and he still hadn't decided but went to university anyway.

Academic is defined as *of, or relating to, institutionalized education and scholarship.* The same word, at the same time, also means *having little practical use or value, as by being overly detailed, unengaging or theoretical.*

The latter definition seemed the most appropriate for Ed's university career which was a mash up of drinking, diving, surfing, kayaking and having his heart-broken. All washed down with a few pints.

After three years of that he was awarded a second class joint honours degree which he put in the recycling bin and went in search of something that would make him feel better.

That trip to Jake and Jayne's place in Florida was close to the beginning of what turned into a decade of globe-trotting and adrenalin-fuelled adventure, going to the places of his dreams and doing exactly what he wanted. So you can perhaps imagine how confused and gutted he was to find that, as the years passed, he was becoming *more* disillusioned with life – until the day when he woke up on an Irish beach (with sand in his mouth) looking at the Atlantic Ocean and knowing he'd reached the end of the road – in every way.

That was last year.

He'd spent the past twelve months living on the cliff-top overlooking that beach, trying to understand how he could have had everything he'd ever wanted in life and still not be happy. What was missing?

Most people talk about a mid-life crisis like it's a specific period of emotional turmoil in middle-age characterised by a strong desire for change probably caused by the realization that they too must grow old and die. Well, Ed envied *most people* and their few years of psychological stress because his own mid-life crisis had been a central question that had coursed through the heart of every moment – sometimes subtle, sometimes shocking – since the day he was born. And likely till the day he died.

Who am I? Where's the point and purpose and meaning?

The only time he felt fully alive was when he was on an edge, risking his life. What's all that about? It was only going to end one way.

Maybe Ed would change his opinion about all this when he hit middle-age. Or it hit him. Perhaps it already had. When is *middle-age*? After all, he could be dead tomorrow.

And so it was, waking up on the beach with sand in his mouth, the question was burying him alive.

Who am I? Where's the point and purpose and meaning?

Sensation seeking just eased things temporarily. Like scratching an itch.

And he didn't want to feel *better* for a few moments he wanted to feel well – and all the time.

That was a year ago.

Living in the cliff-top cabin was a very simple life and, by accident, just under the surface of this simplicity he'd found what he was looking for, which was happiness. No, happiness is the wrong word because modern-world happiness is too often loud and superficial. And fleeting. Ed's discovery was more satisfying and stable than that.

Contentment. The feeling that quietly bubbled away in the background of the ordinary activity of his every day was contentment. He was appreciating simple pleasures.

He'd experienced for himself how mind – his mind – was the root of all his contentment, and all his frustration. And that his own mind was fucked up, and he suffered because of it.

While living this simple existence he was better able to watch his mind and was becoming more proficient in (and quite proud of) the ability to identify and disengage from disturbing thoughts and emotions, and thereby transform his moods. He was living proof that if you made enough wrong turns you could still end up heading in the right direction.

So when he received an invitation to attend a wedding at an exclusive English hotel it seemed like the perfect opportunity for a bit of excitement, and to road test this new self.

And Tracy would be there. Ed had not seen Tracy for ages.

The ferry crossing was smooth. Ed spent a lot of time on deck, his gaze on the horizon where the sky met the Irish Sea, just like his Atlantic back on the cliff top. He exhaled. Aaaaah... This was going to be fun.

His plan was to hitch to England on the M4. Easy.

His first lift was with a delivery driver who needed to talk. Ed said how he'd travelled a lot and the driver asked him where he'd been. When Ed listed *Florida* Delivery Driver's eyes lit up.

"Me too! I've been by-there, Orlando, brilliant! Did you go to Disneyland?

"No."

"Sea World?"

"Uh, no."

"Kennedy Space Centre then? "

"Nope."

"Key West? Delray Beach?..."

Now Delivery Driver was really anxious. *I've listed all the places you go to when you go to Florida and this lying lunatic has been to none of them – this is probably the first time he's crossed the Severn Bridge. At least he's going to England, he'll fit in better over there.*

Ed realised he had unnerved Delivery Driver so gently offered an explanation: how he and Tracy had been staying with an American friend who lived in an area of Florida not frequented by tourists.

"But this Tracy is a bloke, right?" clarified Delivery Driver.

"Right."

"So?" said The Delivery Driver uncomfortable with a few seconds of silence.

"So what?"

"Did you?"

"Did I what?"

"Did you get to Canada?"

They had just gone through the tunnel at Newport. Delivery Driver was dropping Ed in Chepstow which was maybe thirty minutes down the road and finishing the story, controlling the conversation, would probably be the most relaxing way to spend the time...

frontier

The Heavy Chevy broke down for the final time within view of the little town of Nohope in which was located the only salvage yard for hundreds of miles. They rolled the heroic car in through the gates but Salvage Man wasn't interested until the lads pointed out it was nearly full of petrol and had a case of beer in the trunk.

That made it worth $25.

They took the money then removed their tent, packs and the case of beer from the car and walked next door, to the only shop in Nohope, where they selected a postcard of a big empty prairie and *'Nohope, Saskatchewan, Canada'* written in yellow letters along the bottom.

"Dear Ronald…"

They discussed their next move while drinking the beer in the tent pitched on the prairie (that looked just like the prairie on the post-card).

Ed liked the idea of Alaska, he always had done. It cured Dr Fleischmann in *Northern Exposure*, maybe it could remedy whatever malaise was troubling him.

Tracy listened to Ed's plan. Nah. Wishy-washy soul-searching didn't really appeal. Tracy was going to Vancouver to check out the grunge music scene.

They decided to play spoof for their tent. Ed won but he didn't want the tent. Neither did Tracy. So they left it on the prairie at Nohope.

Ed woke up. It had been no ordinary sleep. Maybe he'd been hit over the head? It was broad daylight. He was outside. There were lots of people milling about. He was fully clothed. He was in a sleeping bag. His backpack was next to him. He was on a sun lounger. All the other sun loungers – there was a long line of them – were empty. The sky was overcast, the air was cold.

There was a line of people wrapped up in coats with their backs to him looking over a wall. The wall was a gunwale, the floor was a deck, he was on a boat. His bladder was about to pop.

He found a toilet then walked around looking for Tracy. On his third loop he stopped at the cafeteria. People were speaking English, but there was a faraway feel. For example, no real tea bags. He spent a lot of money on a cup of hot water and dunked a tea-bag in it and jiggled it about. The water went green. He looked at his watch. Four in the afternoon. He was gradually coming out of the fog and arriving at an explanation for Now. One piece at a time he pieced it all together.

Tracy was still sleeping when Ed had crawled out of the tent in Nohope. Ed had felt freedom, put his thumb in the air and spent four days on the road. This boat was the Prince Rupert ferry to Alaska, it was part of the plan, there was nothing sinister going on – always a relief.

He looked at his watch again. It was Tuesday.

Next he remembered stealing a few hours sleep under a porta-cabin in a town called Hinton at the foot of the Rocky Mountains. It was daylight for half the night and very cold. The ice on his bivvy bag crackled as he wriggled out of it. In the gas station café he drank a cup of strong, hot coffee. It was like engine oil. When he felt his system turning over and the blood returning to his forehead, fingers and toes he accepted a top-up and, cradling the precious mug, looked for wisdom out of the window.

A warm-looking car drove passed him. He put his hand back in his pocket and shivered. A trucker who had been having breakfast emerged from the café, saw him standing there and whistled.

Ed was going to ride across the Rockies in the cab of an

eighteen-wheeler, on a clear day, at sunrise. Neat. But as soon as he was on board his next worry took over; would he get to Prince Rupert in time to catch this week's ferry up the world famous 'Inside Passage' to Alaska? So, when he should have been enjoying a once-in-a-lifetime experience of crossing The Rockies in a truck at sunrise, he was already up the inside passage.

Alaska is on a scale all on its own, even Canadians agree. The ferry takes two days and nights to get as far as Skagway which is still only half way to Anchorage.

But Ed knew the nature of ultra-distance wilderness hitch-hiking; there would only be a few cars but almost all of them would be going all the way. So he only needed one ride, or maybe two.

He also knew that when the ferry docked he needed to be ready on the road with his thumb out as the car deck emptied. He went to the exit stairwell an hour before arrival so he could be one of the first foot passengers off.

One by one the cars drove off the ferry and up the ramp towards him. There were brand new hire cars containing anxious looking couples, four-wheel drive mobile homes dripping with expedition accessories and all-terrain jeeps driven by lonely-looking rustic occupants wearing tartan shirts. Ed wondered if he would have the courage to accept a lift if he was offered one.

He needn't have worried, one after another they drove up the ramp towards him, and passed him, until the stream of traffic slowed and dried up all together.

Just him and the dusty road.

What now?

He walked to edge of town – which was not very far – there was nobody around. He stood and waited. And waited.

In the ditch on the other side of the road, there was a gutter pipe sticking out of the ground. It was about fifteen metres away.

There was some gravel by his feet. This could help pass the time. He would throw little stones – one at time – until he got one in the pipe, which could be days, which could be how long he'd be standing there.

He threw the first stone, it looped across the road in the direction of the pipe. Looking good...he heard the hollow rattle as it descended into the pipe.

The first stone, just like that.

He dropped the handful of gravel.

What now?

There was a buzzing in the distance like a giant mosquito. No, a car was coming, and it stopped for Ed!

The man was big, his car was very small. The engine could have been from a sewing machine.

"Good on fuel is it?" asked Ed

"No idea mate. I got off the same ferry as you, I only just bought it."

"Are you working, or is this just a road-trip or something?" asked Ed

"I got a court summons."

"Oh, okay. What's your name?"

"Shane."

It never got dark and they never stopped driving.

A week later Ed saw Shane on the steps of the courthouse in Seward and shouted out to him. Shane ignored him. Ed approached calling Shane – no response – Shane was not his real name.

People go to Alaska to connect with nature and commune with themselves. Ed was finding out it would be better to do that before you travel otherwise the beauty and the bigness will quickly undo you.

Three weeks after arriving in Alaska, having been denied work in every place he had tentatively applied, Ed turned for "home".

He got a ride with a guy who introduced himself as Jerry the Halibut King, or alternatively The Halibut Guru, because he held the world record for the biggest halibut ever caught with a rod and line. Ever.

Until recently that is.

Recently a grandmother on a charter boat had hooked a halibut the size of a small whale, so while Jerry was still known as The Halibut King it wasn't the same. He was a king without a kingdom and was struggling with this new non-sense of identity.

I mean, after all, this was not just some world heavyweight boxing crown where you learn from your mistakes, train harder and smarter, challenge for a rematch and retain the title. If only it were that easy.

The chances of Jerry ever being a champion again were so slim. Halibut so rarely grow that big, and even if an equally huge specimen did exist, there are so many other fish in the sea.

That was part of it.

The other aspect which Jerry was finding difficult to digest was the agent of his obscurity. If he had been relieved of his title by one of his burly fishing buddies who had also dedicated their life to halibut angling, well, that would be disappointing but at least there would be honour in it. And respect for the fish. But to be stripped of his credentials by an old woman tourist…

Remembering this, Ed was struck by the incredible ways that human beings choose to spend their limited lives. How we dedicate ourselves to the strangest things. Hooking halibut for example. I mean how the hell did that happen? Here's a possibility:

When Jerry was a kid his baseball summer camp was cancelled so he went on a hiking trip with his dad but the weather was too bad to climb a mountain so they chartered a boat and went salmon fishing which is when he caught his first little halibut. His dad clapped him on the shoulder, followed by all the other men on the boat that day. That was Jerry's first taste of man-sized pride, and he kinda liked it.

Halibut have both eyes on one side of their head and from that day on so did Jerry.

But at the time Ed didn't reflect too much on Jerry's lopsided life choices, he was more concerned with putting some space between himself and his own latest embarrassment.

While Jerry could talk he was also a generous listener.

Originally Ed had planned to return to the lower 48 States of America – across half of Alaska and all of Canada – by bicycle. He told Jerry how he had been in the bike shop and selected his new bike and how The Cycle Technician had taken it out the back and was busy fitting a pannier rack and drink bottle holders as well as switching the brakes over (so the left hand was the back brake and the right hand was the front brake, like it is in Europe and everywhere else in the world except America). Meanwhile Cycle Salesman was darting about gathering a small pile of essentials – the pannier bags, a bike pump, puncture repair kit, spare tubes and tyre, drink bottles...

When everything was nearly ready Ed went over to the till to pay. His card was refused. And refused again. There was money on the card, Ed was confused. Cycle Technician and Cycle Salesmen were fuming, they stood over Ed as he shouldered his pack and backed out the door.

In retrospect, there was no rational explanation *except* Ed's Guardian Angel had intervened – it was time to get his boy out of there.

If that bike shop transaction had gone through Ed would have been an old man before he got to Canada or, more likely, a not-so-beautiful corpse on the side of the Alcan Highway.

Ed winced at the thought. Soul-searching can go on too long. Can become an identity in itself.

Ed's next lift came along almost as soon as he stuck out his thumb, courtesy of Chris, a lad of his own age. Chris had been packed off to Alaska by his father "to make a man of himself".

"So, Daisy – see you in a year or two," his father had said.

Chris had lasted just three weeks (the same as Ed), now he was heading home, all the way to Chicago, 3,500miles.

They drove non-stop. When Ed tried to sleep Chris would swerve and scream, Ed would sit bolt upright in shock and Chris would laugh.

Yeah, Haha.

When Ed was driving he preferred to just let Chris sleep.

Gas stations were at least a few hundred miles apart with nothing in between. On one occasion when they stopped for fuel Chris filled the tank then reached in the open window, took some dollar bills from his wallet and dropped it back on the seat next to Ed. It contained his remaining cash, all of his cards and his driving license. The keys were in the ignition.

Ed slipped into the driver's seat and drove the car around the side of the gas station and waited for Chris to emerge.

He watched Chris cross the forecourt to the car which wasn't there. Even from that distance he could see Chris' face move from shock to disbelief into despair and then fear. Ed gave him another few seconds of thinking through the implications of being left in the middle of nearly-nowhere while his identity and everything he owned was being driven away in his car by a guy whose name could be Ed who may come from Wales which is next to England but not part of England but still part of the British Isles... before he whistled at Chris.

Chris walked over. Ed threw the keys back to him.

"Don't fuck with me, Daisy." During the next stretch Ed got some sleep.

The customs man at the Alaska-to-Canada border was born to be a customs man. If he was a woman, he would have been a customs man. If he was a dog he would have been a sniffer dog.

He got pleasure out of messing with people and it appeared to be at his discretion how much cash travellers needed to re-enter Canada.

Slowly the facts were becoming clear.

Ed had enough money, just.

Chris didn't have enough.

Credit cards were no good, just cash.

It was a Thursday evening before a bank holiday weekend.

There was a bank just across the border but they were being refused entry.

The nearest bank on the Alaskan side was more than one day's drive back the way they had come.

Being sent back and hanging out until the banks next opened on Tuesday morning would be expensive.

Customs Man was refusing to let them through.

Chris protested. Customs Man sent them away harder.

Chris and Ed went back to the car and talked – boy to boy – about their predicament.

"I have enough cash and a card, I could hitch from here," said Ed.

"I don't have enough cash," said Chris ,"and on my own I couldn't afford the gas to drive back to the bank, which would be a waste of time anyway because there is no money left on my card. And it's not as if I can call my dad."

"I have enough cash and a card, I could hitch from here," Ed repeated.

"Yes, but, *If* you left me here, and *if* you got picked up, it would be by a lonely and deranged, gun-toting, red-neck, welsh-rarebit-eating son of a bitch!"

If the roles were reversed Ed was sure that Chris would already be thumbing his way into Canada. But Ed was occasionally plagued with a sense of morality, and right then he was suffering from a bout. But what to do?

Once, following a passionate remonstration at an airport check-in desk Ed had moved himself from the waiting list to Business Class on a trans-Atlantic flight. They had no choice; he would have to employ similar tactics.

Ed composed himself. Tears were the easy bit, the key was hitting the right level of sincerity and intensity without crossing the line into instability and liability. All he had to do was focus on the facts. And embellish them a small bit.

While Ed got into character Chris made a pipe out an empty Coke can and went almost out of sight to smoke the last of his pot.

Twenty minutes earlier Customs Man had been diminutive in stature, now he stood towering over a six-foot tall bearded hippy who was listing the series of misfortunes that had befallen him while sobbing in a semi-controlled fashion.

Customs Man was used to facing boys who had travelled to The Last Great Frontier thinking they were bigger than the wild, or that they *are* the wild. And they needed to be taught a lesson.

Ed could see he was getting nowhere but he couldn't give up…

"It's just my family, if I miss the reunion *and* the wedding… (still no reaction from Customs man)…I am always only just a disappointment to them(oh…oh…that struck a nerve…), I never did as well as my brothers and sisters at anything so if I screw this up too…(bingo!)"

Customs Man decided to throw out the rule book, and go with The Bottom Line. The Bottom Line in decisions like this has nothing to do with right or wrong. It's all about *the come back*. Customs Man had to decide if letting these lads into Canada would cause him and his career any trouble. Would it come back to bite him on the butt?

As soon as they were out of sight on the Canadian side of the border Ed pulled over. He was trembling. Method acting is a demanding business especially when it's not acting. There had not been a director in the shadows ready to shout "Cut. Let's have another go at that one."

Ed had had to nail it first time. He'd poured a lot into the last few minutes and was still *in-character* so to speak, and yes, he was feeling it for real.

Meanwhile, in the passenger seat, Chris couldn't feel anything. He'd smoked a month's pot in one hit.

◆

"Chris couldn't feel anything. In fact I checked for a pulse, he'd smoked a month's pot in one hit you see." said Ed as Delivery Driver pulled into a lay-by just after the *Chepstow* sign.

Ed thanked him and put out a hand, Delivery Driver hesitated for a moment before shaking it. He put the van in first gear and drove off before Ed could shut the door behind him.

It was a good place to hitch from, between two round-abouts so the traffic was slow moving, and with a bus shelter if the weather turned dirty.

Without waiting very long a truck pulled over. Ed climbed in. Truck Driver was quiet, even when he was talking. And smiled, even when he was talking. Ed listened, or talked, and smiled back. But most of the time it was just the noise of the engine and the wind and the wheels on the road, which gave Ed time to reflect.

The contrast in energies of Delivery Driver and Truck Driver was striking. Delivery Driver was getting to a place so he could make his delivery. The driving was *the nuisance bit* that had to happen in between making his deliveries. Then it was more bloody driving.

Truck Driver drove his truck. He liked it, and that's what he did.

It didn't make a difference where he was going or what he was carrying, either way his job was driving, accelerating up through the gears and braking and turning and parking and stopping. Arriving and leaving.

Contentment, Ed decided, was the difference between Delivery Driver and Truck Driver. If you want to be happy you have to enjoy what you do.

Simple.

So why is it so difficult?

Ed had spent his life de-valuing almost everything he did in 'Delivery-Driver style'. He de-valued almost everything by relating to it as a stepping stone to *The Real Thing* – whatever the hell that was.

He shopped so he could cook. He cooked so he could eat. He ate so he had energy. He needed energy to do stuff which made him hungry again. He never got to *The Real Thing*. He ran his theory by Truck Driver.

"Maybe," said Trucker while smiling. And driving.

Next Ed found himself standing at the side of a slip road onto the M4 near Swindon, the cars were already travelling fast as they passed. It would be difficult for them to pull over here even if they wanted to. He was sure most of them didn't even see him. The cars were mostly big, usually with just one pale person inside; while accelerating they were steering, changing gear, drinking coffee, eating pasties (or filled rolls), talking on mobile phones and reaching into a pocket or adjusting the AC.

Wow. Nobody does only one thing at a time any more. This was a world away from his cliff-top in Ireland. It mesmerised him, flashing by, engines powered by the Have-Not mentality. Everyone trying to make a buck off everyone else. Selling our products to make money so we can buy shit we don't need.

"...the insistent clamour of that disgusting god, money." wrote Everett Reuss.

Too busy to count our blessings. Or even be aware of them.

Surely, never before in the history of humankind, has *my will* so universally overshadowed and out-boxed *thy will.* And none of us are happy. It's not working. It's time for some collective honesty on this. And peer support to change the way we live.

If one at a time, but as soon as possible, we all slowed down and learned to relax, and cooperate rather than compete, the whole world would be a lot happier. And richer. And our salvation would be a lot closer.

Isn't it?

Ed gave up. That is to say he still had his thumb out, but he let the cars pass without giving them a second thought. Or even an initial thought. The cars came, and they went, just like before, but he wasn't following them, thinking after them, he was letting them go.

He became very spacious; rising thoughts were mere clouds in his sky-like mind. He let them pass. He remained on the spot, in the moment. Thought free. Content.

Do we have to be falling before we grow wings? It was a passing thought. One that appealed to him. He followed it. The moment was over. Time began again. Cars whizzed by, piloted by pale people living their extreme existence.

And the thoughts came bumper-to-bumper too; there is something so deadening about a shirt-and-tie commute to a job that begins and ends at the same time each day and has a fixed monthly salary.

It's the comfort and security we all thought we wanted. But it's a false comfort and fake security. It's a certain kind of certainty. The illusion of control which makes the surprises, when they come, so uncomfortable.

Cruel even.

Right now Ed's life was an open-ended journey. He was very openly and obviously at the mercy of the elements, and the subject of other people's generosity. And spite.

He was attracted to this edge of unknowing, of hope and fear, he instinctively knew that surfing it was precondition for growth and transformation. And for feeling alive. Waking up and going out into the world not knowing what each day would hold, taking life as it comes, relinquishing any illusion of control. That's fresh, that's a good morning!

His inspiration in this was Siddhartha who was born a prince, grew up in the King's palace and as a young man enjoyed social status, political power material possessions and, of course, a hareem of delightful dancing girls.

Yet still Siddhartha was unsatisfied. So unsatisfied that at the age of twenty nine he renounced it all, left the palace, cut his hair, switched clothes with a poor shepherd and, overnight, went from the king's kitchen to the scraps in his begging bowl. And yes, through that, in time, he found not only his contentment but the purpose and meaning of human being!

Ed's attention shifted back to the traffic before his eyes, the senseless chase for material goods that has replaced the more essential pursuit of spiritual happiness.

Ed was following Siddhartha's example; the focus was making

the spirit strong rather than making one's self comfortable. But Ed's version of being a Wandering Yogi was the toy version. Yes, he was currently unemployed, squatting in a remote cabin and had recently shaved off his dreads, but he still had a credit card in his back pocket which removed him from the full experience – he may as well be wearing a suit of armour.

For example; if Siddhartha was hitching to a wedding and he got a bit tight for time, Siddhartha would not have gone into a service station and called a taxi. Which is what Ed did.

threshold

Ed had £21 in cash (and the credit card in his back pocket of course).

"How far are we from hotel?" he asked

"The turn is coming up soon." replied the taxi driver "But the entrance road goes on for a few miles."

"You can pull over here," said Ed. The meter was at £19.50. Ed handed him a twenty, got out of the car, slung his jacket over his shoulder and started walking.

His whistle echoed as he walked through the arch of an imposing gatehouse. He continued up an avenue of majestic trees, the sun blinked through leaves that danced in the summer breeze. The world was reflecting his mood back at him.

Cars passed; big cars with dark windows and fast cars with small windows. And a leather-clad lunatic on a white motorbike who, using the last inch of tarmac, overtook a car that was overtaking Ed. The biker slowed long enough to appreciate a huge garden sculpture before roaring on around the corner.

The hotel had five stars and an indoor arboretum. Helicopters were landing and leaving. Photographers from Hello magazine were in the car park. No-one paid any attention to Ed. Why would they, he was obviously just lost. Or late for work.

Ed had gone to school with the groom; they had climbed trees together. Now the friend was at the top of the corporate ladder. His bride had been in a girl band before becoming Britain's top model.

Ed liked extreme, craved it, but his version of extreme was adrenalin fuelled adventure, and more recently living without electricity in a cabin on a cliff-top at the western edge of western Europe with only the sheep and sea-gulls for company. Today was an unfamiliar and uncomfortable extreme. But hey, no problem. He had changed, he was different now, he had a self-confidence that was based on personal insights and a profound understanding of the nature of reality. He no longer looked outside himself for affirmation, no longer handed that power to others.

What a crock of shit! He was a wreck. His cliff-top equipoise was a million miles away and he would do anything to be back there now; to watch the waves whiten on the rocks and the gulls tease the on-shore breeze.

Ed watched another helicopter land and drained his champagne in time to switch it for a full glass as the waiter passed. He was having anxiety apnea. Just two weeks before he had cut off his dreads, didn't need that badge any more. How wrong he was! The hair had been his introduction and explanation. He was naked without his stories. He was naked now.

He must remember to breathe. When people started going inside. He stayed outside. Wondered about leaving.

Where the hell was Tracy?

tracy

Tracy had loved metalwork in school – he was a highly skilled machinist – nowadays we would call him a geek but back then the word was 'gifted'. He won a top apprenticeship with a prestigious company which led into a well-paid career manufacturing precision parts. At the trade fair his future employers had told him he would be playing an important role in keeping his country safe and secure. His starting salary was more than his dad had ever earned, he would have a security pass and wear overalls with his name embroidered onto them.

And so it was; while most of his friends were attending endless interviews or faffing around between college courses he had bought a house and owned a race-tuned Kawasaki.

Until one Monday morning (he had cried himself to sleep the night before and wasn't sure why), while sitting on the pot with a toothbrush in his mouth, he suddenly fully realised what he did for a living. Which was make washers for nuclear warheads. His job was manufacturing weapons of mass destruction! Vomit and toothpaste froth splashed onto the tiles. He gave himself a minute, wiped his butt, stepped out of his overalls (used them to mop the floor and dropped them out of the window), washed his hands, saw evil in the mirror and had a meltdown.

He painted his front door black and kept the curtains closed. Once a week his mother came round to clean. A few select friends were allowed to visit – if they brought cigarettes, hated conversation and were good at Playstation. They each had a key to get in because Tracy rarely got off the sofa. His mother made appointments with the full spectrum of specialists, he missed most of them and mystified the rest. He was beyond redemption. How do you rescue such incandescent karma? Simple. You don't.

His real name was Spencer Tracy Evans but Spencer was the one who did as he was told and wiped whole populations off the world map. He needed to get as far away from Spencer as he possibly could. From that time onwards he called himself Tracy and lived behind the black door.

Occasionally, on winter afternoons when it was dark already, Tracy would slink out to have his head shaved, or get another tattoo or have something else pierced. It was who he was and how he felt. Inhospitable, dangerous, bereft. None of it was for effect. If he wanted to shock he put on a clean woollen jumper, a beanie and black rim spectacles.

"It's the super-man effect." he explained to Ed.

"The super what?"

"The specs look nerdy but it's implied nerdness. To imply nerdness it is necessary to be anything but a nerd."

"Yeaaah," said Ed unconvinced. "Yeaaah, but, if I was meeting you for the first time how would I know if you were an authentic nerd or just pretending."

"Because Scrambles, a real nerd would giggle awkwardly and back off whereas I would kick the living shit out of you."

Which was another plus for changing his name from Spencer to Tracy.

He got into more fights.

It was Ed who finally pulled Tracy out his his vortex of self-destruction. It was an accident, Ed didn't mean to help, and if Tracy had realised what was happening he would have resisted it because hating-the-world is quite a satisfying and easy position to take.

So Tracy's epiphany was thanks to Ed but completely unintentional and it happened like this. Ed was just back from a year river-guiding in Nepal and happened to mention to Tracy that the UK was the most expensive place in the world to buy cigarettes. That was it! Helping to build the British Government's nuclear arsenal had irreparably damned Tracy's soul, now he was being unfairly taxed to give himself a list of cancers!

There was not much to do; he'd recently crashed the Kawasaki in a thinly veiled attempt to kill himself so he put his house with the black front door on the market, packed a bag and followed Ed to Nepal.

Tracy thought Ed was an irritating hippy fuckwit. Tracy was right. But Ed had adventures and unwittingly, without being the least bit brave or bold, had a curious ability to get himself into trouble, and out of it again, before trouble even knew it had been violated. This intrigued Tracy, he admired it as an alternative form of aggression. He called Ed's attribute *The Audacity Shield*.

shield

Ed had hooked up with Pen and Kim who had just finished a year of study at the University of Illinois.

"Study, hah! Did you know that at American Universities you can take Frisbee Throwing as a module."

It was the summer break so eleven of them went to Chicago for the weekend. It was an international group but predominantly Australian and, after taking a double room in the The Lakeside Hotel, they called themselves *Lake's Eleven*.

Pen and Mike (the most trustworthy looking pair in the group) had checked in to the room, the rest of the mob filtered in up the stairs or via the lift in ones and twos. The shower was running for nearly two hours before everybody was ready to go out on the town.

During the night the group split leaving Ed, Pen, Mike and Jan lost, wandering the dark streets looking for the hotel. Finally they saw the neon lights of Kingston Mines, the blues club they had left an hour earlier. They'd walked in a big circle!

There was a taxi at the kerb. The driver was leaning against his car, he saw them approaching, turned, fumbled with the door handle, jumped in his car and shut the door quickly. Ed approached the window. Taxi Driver opened it a very small bit. Ed asked the way to The Lakeside, how far it was and if it was safe to walk?

The driver heard the accent and wound the window right down and laughed like only a fatman can.

"Safe? Safe! Hey mother fucker, if you just came from that direction, and at this time of the night, you can go anywhere in this city!"

They decided to take the taxi anyway and Ed had thought nothing more of it until he happened to mention this early hours jaunt through South Side Chicago to Tracy.

"See! See! And you were wearing pink board shorts and a bandana?... " he threw his hands up in the air with delight because he, like anybody, loves to have their theories proved right. "...Imagine all the hoodlums and muggers, gangsters and pimps standing in doorways and alleys and looking out from first floor windows, watching you all pass in your beach gear and hippy threads, thinking *No, something's not right. It must be a trap* and letting you walk on by. See! See!"

Everyone around the table had no idea what exactly they were supposed to be *seeing* because Audacity Shield Theory was a secret. Tracy didn't want to share it with anyone in case they started inventing stories that would skew the data.

Tracy took up the narrative with another example; the

lunchtime drinking session in a seaside town in Cornwall. This time Tracy was there, so it was an eye-witness account.

They had found a string of great pubs and were enjoying themselves so much they missed lunch. Later in the afternoon Ed got peckish so went in search of a custard slice. All he could find was an excellent pasty shop. Three pasties and a-nice-chat-with-the-baker later he made his way back to the pub only to find his mates prostrate in the car-park dripping blood. Some locals had hired a gang of bikers to beat them up.

Tracy was delighted. Two of his favourite things had happened. He'd been outnumbered in a fight *and* Ed's Audacity Shield had proved itself – again.

"He was only gone fourteen minutes and he missed it!"

But that was not the end of it. By closing time they were too wasted to walk up the long and winding hill to their host's house – maybe just this once they would drive.

Everyone piled into the back of Ed's 1967 bay window VW van and prepared for take off.

Pulling out of the car park Ed wiped the condensation off the windscreen with his jacket sleeve while the front seat passenger cranked up the stereo so the van was rocking as it rolled slowly up and around the first two bends. Which is when they saw the road block and flashing lights. Ed looked in his rear-view mirror and saw more squad cars.

There were flashing lights in front of them and flashing lights behind.

They were boxed in. It was a sting.

"We're fucked!" they all said in unison, then they told each other to shut-the-fuck-up. Ed turned the stereo off and opened his window to let the smoke out and some fresh air in. In the side-view mirror he saw the approaching uniformed officer. Then he looked in the rear-view mirror at the boys taking a deep breath and burying themselves under sleeping bags.

A year before Ed had been walking between pubs in a city somewhere in England and relieved himself against an emergency exit of a Tesco supermarket. He span around as he zipped himself up, ready to chase after the group, and was looking into the eyes of a pair of police people.

He didn't think about running or blagging. There really was no point. He placed one wrist on top of the other and said "It's a fair cop". Factually. Without any hint of condescension.

They let him go.

Another time, for another reason, he did get bundled into the back of the police van but just as they were shutting the doors they got an emergency call. They pushed him out again and sped off.

Now, drunk at the helm of his overloaded vehicle, he was face-to-face with the law again. The police person's torch was blinding. He thought about getting his wrists ready for cuffing like any self-respecting citizen would, but he didn't. That sort of luck doesn't happen twice. People hide when they've got something to hide, Ed decided to speak first.

"Evenin' offisser. Whassat smell? "

"Yes sir, sorry about this. Road's closed. There's a restaurant kitchen on fire," said the policeman.

"Ouch, okay. I'll switch my engine off, will I?"

"I would, sir."

Another oft quoted example of Ed's unwitting ability to cheat prison and/or grievous bodily harm and/or death was when, on the road to Darjeeling, a Merlon saved his life.

merlon

Ed had to go to India to renew his Nepalese visa. He left Kathmandu two days later than planned – delayed by the string of parties in the run up to the Christmas break, and was travelling by bicycle – so he finally arrived at the Indian border five days after his visa expired.

Many people had happily shared stories of their own nightmare experiences – and others they'd heard on the grapevine – of hassle at the border if you overstay your visa. "They deffo won't let you back in."

Ed was employed as a river guide in Nepal, so getting out without a black mark so he could get back in two weeks later was important to him...

He had been cycling for three very long days when he arrived at the Indian border town called Raniganj. He knew the first step to avoiding trouble is not to worry about it. Luckily he was too wasted to worry, or even have a coherent thought. He was caked in dust, a bit shivery and needed to lie down.

The two border guards had nothing to do. They would have plenty of time to get to the bottom of this. One of them took his passport, looked at it, looked at him, looked at it, turned to the visa page, looked at him, looked at it, pulled a face and gave it to his colleague. Who went through the same routine. No-one had said anything yet. It was very quiet. Then a third man in uniform came in the front door, he was whistling and carrying a tray with three cups of chai and a big bowl of samosas. He looked at Ed and started laughing. He said something to his colleagues and they all had a good laugh. The third man put the tray of food down and made pedal motions with his hands, then pointed to the door where Ed's bike was leaned against the wall. The reprobate standing in front of them had cycled from Nepal.

"Yeah..." Ed said dredging up a smile and making peddle motions with his hands.

They took Ed's dollars – more than he had been expecting – and stamped his passport and then got on with their supper.

All the restaurants were closed but Ed found a guest house. The boy will bring you soup they said. The room was a concrete cell, in the corner was a tap and a drain hole. Next to that was a bucket with an electric coil standing in it.

He heated the water in the bucket while he drank the soup. He stood over the drain hole and upturned the bucket of warm water over his head.

Flaking paint from the roof lay on the top bunk, and it was too high up anyway. He dropped into the lower bunk.

Two days later, in the early evening, Ed arrived at The Himalaya Guesthouse and Café in Darjeeling. He was given a key and directions to his room. The door was already unlocked, he went in, the television was on.

"Hello?"

"You're late. Eight fucking days late!" said a familiar voice. Tracy was sitting up in bed surrounded by half-written post-cards and half-eaten bags of crisps and an open bottle of coke. He was wearing a balaclava.

"What's wrong with you?"

"I got the screaming hab-dabs and a fever." Tracy snivelled.

Ed had a cut above his eye and a grazed chin but Tracy didn't take his eyes off the women in swimsuits who were dancing on the TV.

Ed limped over to the second bed and was asleep before the song finished.

He was woken by the *adhan* calling Muslims to prayer, which struck him as odd. There was a Bible on the table next to his bed and His Holiness the Dalai Lama, the world's most famous Buddhist, lived up the road. Three major religions existing peacefully in the same town? If they can live together here why can't they do it in the rest of the world? Perhaps it was a dream. There was blood on his pillow. He turned it over and fell asleep again.

There was no hot water for a shower so Ed and Tracy went downstairs and ordered two breakfasts with tea. A minute later the tea arrived.

"Oh, excuse me, sorry," said Ed. "sorry, excuse me, ahem, this is coffee."

"I know, we're out of tea," said the waitress as she walked away.

"Oh. Okay."

"That's pretty fuckin funny isn't it?" said Tracy without a hint of humour.

"What?"

"Scrambles, we're in a café. In India. *In Darjeeling.* And they've got no tea!"

It was funny, but smiling hurt Ed's jaw.

"What happened to you anyway?" said Tracy.

"I fell off my bike."

"I'm not your mother. You can tell me the truth."

"It is true."

Ed had been unlucky. The road to Darjeeling is nearly all uphill but on one of the few steep descents he'd hit a deep pothole – more like a bomb crater – that was lurking in the shadows on a sharp bend. He was pinged into the air before rolling across the broken tarmac and, on the outside of the bend, he collided with a concrete parapet built to stop things going over the edge and into the ravine. His bike bounced and scraped through a gap in the parapets, and dropped out of sight.

He was woken up by someone trying to remove his wallet

from his shorts.

One of his pannier bags was next to him. The other one must be with his bike in the river at the bottom of the valley. He was lucky he'd hit the concrete wall.

"Damn right you were lucky – a merlon saved your life!..." Momentarily Tracy forgot his fever, "...That's what they're called. The sitcky-up bit on the top of a castle wall is a merlon, the gap in between is a crenel. Your bike went through a crenel – you hit a merlon. It was a fifty-fifty chance and a merlon saved your life!"

"Well, I'm glad I've cheered you up."

"You haven't. "

But he had. *How audacit was that!* Tracy smiled wide.

Generally speaking Tracy was making progress. Travel had helped. The constant movement was a comfort to his restless soul – maybe if he kept moving he would stay one step ahead of his negative karma?

There was a commotion on the street outside the café. A bearded man with a red face and dressed in a purple dressing gown was having an animated argument with a woman. Someone entered the café, sidestepping the disagreement and ducking in through the doorway, taking shelter from the emotional downpour on the street.

While the door was open Ed could hear the argument. The red-faced beard-man said "I just want to know why!"

"There is no why. You can't analyse it. It's just how it is." the woman retorted just before the door swung shut again. Her accent was American. The man's gesturing was getting wilder, he was English and his face looked familiar.

"We may as well hang out here until after New Year then," said Tracy without a hint of enthusiasm.

"May as well. Are you going to take the balaclava off while we eat?"

Tracy hesitated before removing the balaclava. He placed it on top of the half-written postcards and shivered.

Ed looked out the window at Kangchenjunga, "Five Treasures of Snow", the third highest mountain in the world. He had some postcards to send too, it was just difficult to know what to write.

Daydreaming is easy but it's always only a temporary escape – and reality is waiting. And Ed's current reality was an extremely posh wedding in England.

gazebo

Ed couldn't find Tracy's name on the seating plan – he must be one of the evening guests – and he couldn't find his own name either. He was causing congestion in the doorway to the function room, the queue was building.

"Did you RSVP?" said a flustered bridesmaid

"Did I wha?"

Suddenly Ed was surrounded by two waistcoats. One took his glass of champagne and put it on a tray. "Please follow me, sir." The other guided him by the elbow which really wasn't necessary – he would have followed that champagne glass anywhere.

The table was large and round. It had a bright white cloth with a feint Celtic pattern on it. And there was a lot of pink. Sashes and runners and napkins. The cutlery was heavy. Real silver.

Ed looked up at his fellow dinner guests, they looked like a Madame Tussauds display; heavy make-up, glassy eyes.

He had been awake most of the previous night and hadn't eaten all day. The food arrived as soon as they were settled; goat's cheese and beetroot salad for the adults and mini gourmet pizzas for the kids – it all looked amazing.

When Ed opened his mouth his taste buds spasmed spraying his food with saliva and spotting the table cloth around his plate.

"Mmmm. Food's good. Those pizzas look pretty neat too. I worked a few winter seasons in Austria, shared a room with a crazy guy who cooked frozen pizzas every night in an old electric oven at the end of the corridor."

Back at the cabin he rarely spoke, silence was a comfort, now it terrified him. His mouth had a mind of it's own. And it raced. Champagne on an empty stomach can do that to you.

"…Anyway, he *always* had frozen pizza which was lucky cos there was only one pan with a lid so I could use that to slow-cook my brown rice…"

He was sure the woman next to him was listening but she didn't look up.

"...the trick with rice is, I learned in Nepal is, don't stir it. Of course you rinse it first and start with cold water – two cups for every cup of rice – and bring it up to the nearly boil before turning it way down and have it gently simmer until all the water is absorbed, but the main point is, the way you can really fuu…y'know, mess it up is by stirring it…Anyway, twenty minutes before it was ready I'd pop in a few florets of broccoli, then ten minutes before it was ready I would crack an egg over the top and season it…"

The woman's face was expressionless. Her daughter was sitting in the next seat along. Ed guessed her age at twelve. Or eleven. There was a piece of five-star gourmet mini-pizza on the end of the daughter's fork, the fork was mid-air, stranded somewhere between the plate and her open mouth.

"Yuk," said the daughter.

The clocks stopped ticking. The Mother swallowed on nothing. Ed's hole was out of control but he kept digging.

"Actually you're right, it was *Yuk* but somehow it did the job. And you know what they say..."

Still no response. Just bowed heads.

"What they say is *hunger is the best sauce!* Yeah, well, anyway, some days I just had frozen pizza with the crazy guy. But I made sure my pizza was on the lower shelf in the oven so it would catch some of his melting cheese!"

He was sure that last bit would at least appeal to the young girl but she had put her knife and fork together, pushed her plate away and folded her arms.

"After a few seasons the oven's electrical circuits were so caked in cheddar it blew up. But did that put him off? No! He spent weeks trying to design his own boil-in-the-bag pizza. What a freaking mess!"

More silence. Except for silver cutlery on fine china. Which was really loud. The other people on the table said occasional quiet things to the person sitting next to them.

Audacity was history. And new-style composure was a distant dream. Ed was lost somewhere in the middle. He was distracted by a conversation two tables away. Not really a conversation – more of a monologue.

"En-rietta, but you can call me Enri. Our Da's idea, naming me was just about the last thing 'e did before 'e fecked off... aaHaaah!" the girl laughed loud like a kookaburra. "I know...I know...synchronicity I calls it," she continued, raising a wine glass in her right hand while her left hand held a napkin in front of her mouth so she could chew and talk at the same time. "My wedding dress 'ad fifty two buttons down the back so, as you can imagine, I needed 'elp getting out of it, and that's 'ow I met my second 'usband...aaHaaah!" She nearly choked as she shrieked another laugh. Her dining companions cowered.

It was chalk and camembert. Ed couldn't stay sitting down in that room any longer. While looking for a toilet he spotted an open window and stuck his head out of it, which is when he saw the gazebo.

After the bathroom he may just see if he can find his way out to that gazebo.

Sitting in the gazebo he was close enough to know the speeches were happening. The food felt good in his stomach, he was sober again now, his gaze rested in the middle distance.

Oh!

That's when he saw himself, how he was like a pyramid, a pyramid standing on its point. It was the perfect image for how he was today, and how he'd lived his life. A pyramid. The wrong way up. Broad shoulders and a puffed out chest, apparently big but with no basis.

A pyramid teetering on its point. A balancing act. A tentative pose. Affectation. Not who I really am. A precarious sense of self giving a false sense of security.

Wow. And it takes so much effort to be this person I am not. And to be consistent in that. And managing the fall-out when I go off track.

Ed marvelled at all the mental and physical activity necessary to maintain such an edifice, such an Ed-face. Every waking moment directed by, and dedicated to, this I-dentity. It was a full-time job. Then at night he would fall asleep and have dreams about it.

In the same way a series of still photos projected in sequence can give the illusion of moving images, a movie, I cobble together apparently infinite snippets of content, qualities and charactersitics to give the impression of reality and solidity.

He saw how this top-heavy situation subsisted on constant rounds of praise and blame, occasional losses and temporary gains, pushing against ignominy and drawn towards fame, grasping at health and fearful of pain.

Pyramid-on-its-point was a propaganda machine. It was his manic *and* his depression. Always busy. Everything. Anything. Whatever. As long as it was not silence. Or stillness. The movement, activity, noise and distraction was all critical because a pyramid-on-its-point is like a spinning top; you stop, you fall – right?

AHa!

At his cabin on the cliff-top, especially in the early days, he had found that silence&stillness&non-thought had been intensely uncomfortable. Now he understood why. It was threatening his on-point personality.

When he slowed up or quietened down he would start to wobble, would feel like falling!

But fall to where? *Who am I if not this?*

More meditation would answer that question – he was sure of it – at last he was on the right track! But rather than celebrate this he berated himself for not finding the answer sooner.

Why had he had not made a connection with meditation during the two years he had spent in Nepal? How could he have lived for twenty four months in the foothills of the Himalayas and missed the main point? All that time between the birthplace of the Buddha and the spiritual fortress of Tibet, with some of the greatest living spiritual masters on the planet as his neighbours, and still for it never to occur to him to look inside himself for answers?

Of course he had excuses. Number one could be the nineteen hour nightmare bus ride sitting next to Tim the Phantom Jester.

◆

Tracy was still sick and shivering. Hovering between his bed and the pot. He was in no hurry to leave Darjeeling. When he was better he'd take the train to Dehli and fly back to Kathmandu.

Ed was on the bus, it had just stopped to let some passengers and their chickens off, the driver was riding the clutch, ready to leave. Only about nineteen hours and he'd be back in Kathmandu. The seats were wooden benches with wooden back rests and very little leg room.

"I should've flown."

On the bright side, one of the few places left unoccupied was the seat next to Ed, at least he would have some extra wiggle room for the night ahead.

Ed was on the bus because the re-entry visa in his second passport was not 100% official and the road entry was easier to blag than at the airport. And because it was cheaper and he enjoyed saving money more than earning it.

"Still, I should've flown."

The door shut and the bus moved off. Just a few wheel revolutions later it stopped and the door opened again. A westerner got on. Ed thought he recognised him.

It was one of those moments when time slows down and everything expands and opens up and amplifies and magnifies. And then implodes.

The bearded man who had just got on the bus was the same bearded man that had been arguing in the street outside *The Himalaya Guest House and Café*. He was not dressed in a purple gown and his face was not burning red but it was definitely him.

What were the odds of this?

India is the second most populous country in the world, more than one billion people. There are thousands of planes, trains, buses and bicycles going in a million directions. But this crazy guy, who speaks his language, gets on this bus, and this bus has fifty seats, but only one of them is empty...

And nineteen hours to Kathmandu...

"I definitely should have flown."

People like Ed would say they are not religious but when the faeces hits the fan and pins them to the wall they put on a mac and goggles and pray with all their heart. Ed faced the window and said a good one.

The seat sagged under the additional weight. Ed looked round. You have to. You can't ignore someone who is squashed against you for nineteen hours. Well you can. He would. But first you have to acknowledge them in order to be clear that you are happier altogether on your own.

"Alreight," said Ed. It was a statement not a question.

"Hello...I'm Tim...I'm having a really shit time..."

Ed was facing the window again, saying another prayer, hoping yer man was striking up a conversation with the caged chickens across the isle. A quick glance back to see and Tim was looking straight at him.

"...a really fucking shit time," added Tim.

Suddenly Ed knew where he had seen him before. He was of course the red-faced beard-man in a purple dressing gown arguing on the main street in Darjeeling, West Bengal, India. But before that, in his previous life, he was the actor who played the phantom jester in the kiddies TV show *Rent-a-Ghost*.

This had to be a joke.

What kind of karma was coming back to haunt him now?

Tim had spent six months meditating on top of a mountain. During this solitary retreat his fiancé, Lilibeth, was preparing his meals and leaving them outside the door of his hut. As time went by the menu got less imaginative, some days it wasn't cooked properly or seemed to be thrown at the plate. Initially

Tim reasoned that the food was the same it was just because *he* was becoming more fussy and critical. After all, in the bare environment of a solitary retreat there are few distractions, it's easy to fixate and obsess about everything and anything. So not surprising then, that food had become the focus of his judgemental mind.

Tim also knew that a Yogi brings all circumstances, wanted or unwanted, into their meditation. It's called integration. He explained to Ed that when one learns to apply the Buddhist teachings in one's daily activity is when it stops being a philosophy and becomes a way of life.

But this food issue intensified; he started getting a very hard boiled egg for breakfast and half-cooked plain rice for supper. And then one day nothing. No breakfast. And no dinner.

Tim didn't sleep that night, or the next night, and when there was no breakfast on the third day, and no note of explanation, Tim put the Buddha's teachings on integration back on the shelf, broke his retreat, and went to look for something to eat. And then for Lilibeth.

He found her on the main street in Darjeeling, outside The Himalaya Guesthouse and Café. She had some news. While Tim was in retreat she had met someone else. An Indian man who was seven years younger than she was. And they were married.

And she was pregnant.

Ed had to agree that sounded like a good definition of *having a really shit time.*

He looked at his watch. It was eighteen hours and twenty-one minutes to Kathmandu – depending on traffic.

It was dark and he was really tired, but you would have to be dead to have slept on that bus. There was Tim and his bleeding heart, the hard seat and the noise and the fumes and the pot holes. The driver didn't hit *all* the pot-holes, he swerved wildly and managed to miss a few. But potholes were not the only hazard, pedestrians also use the road and too often there are fatalities. In such a case there would be an animated debate between the driver and the family or friends of the deceased, together with any passers-by who had witnessed the accident, and then the bus passengers would get involved, expressing their concern at the delay until, finally, the body would be carried away and the journey would continue.

But what the driver really needed to avoid was a collision with a cow. Because cows are a symbol of wealth, strength, abundance and selfless giving – and they are sacred. So if the driver kills a cow he's arrested.

Nineteen hours is a long journey, tough on the driver. To keep himself awake he would lean on the horn and turn up the volume of his favourite Bollywood soundtrack so he could sing along.

In the interests of safety the bus company provide a 'wing man', usually a boy, who stands at the driver's shoulder to be an extra pair of eyes, peering into the black void beyond the limited scope of the headlights.

Whenever the bus stopped in a village Wing Boy would run to buy another mini-liquor bottle from the nearest snack shack to keep his driver-supervisor on top of his game.

There are no street lights so it was pitch black and the cows don't wear reflective vests or head-torches so often Bus Driver and Wing Boy saw the cows really late which meant a sudden and sharp change of direction, often over some serious potholes, maybe towards a crowd of people.

After an hour or two of this, for most people, it becomes quite banal. But Tim was wide-eyed and wired, he screamed and blasphemed every time.

"Meditation let me down man. I never used to be this neurotic. I'm gonna enjoy myself in Nay-pal. I'm gonna go white-water rafting. Do you know anything about rafting in Nay-pal?"

"Nepal? Rafting? Er, no."

Ed's eyes closed, his head rocked on a jelly-neck, then another brake-and-slide, his face banged off the window glass followed Tim's rant ringing in his right ear...

◆

Mmmm...

Now Ed had some off-the-grid retreat experience of his own so he had more understanding and empathy for Tim. Injured innocence is a very powerful opportunity to see the rising sense of self, so an unfaithful spouse would surely be fantastic fuel, perfect to fan those flames, a great excuse for The Voice to be loud and proud.

Because, in the early days on his cliff-top, whenever Ed had accidentally found himself sitting quietly he became aware of a neurotic voice his head. He assumed that silence&stillness&non-thought was causing The Voice, and that activity silenced it, so he hid in activity.

It was only after a few weeks of living simply and quietly that he realised The Voice was always there, had always been there, but that he only became aware of it in the silence and stillness of meditation.

It was The Voice that kept his pyramid on point. How had he ever let this imposter take such a grip of him?

He gave that some thought now. In the beginning The Voice was a whispered word. Not so much a word as a question. *The* question. The one which had denied his soul any rest. It was the original pointy brick upon which his whole upside down persona was constructed.

Who am I?

The answer was not immediate or easy so, like all fellow human beings, Baby Ed had panicked. Rather than blast the question wide open he coated it with solutions. He didn't know the answer so he made one up. And another one, and another one...

He pieced together figments of experience and imagination, embryonic beliefs and doubts and hopes and fears which all grew arms and legs and lungs. There was once a time, perhaps, when his-story was just a whisper and could have been squished under the heel of a boot, but now it had teeth and testicles.

Now, in the gazebo, reflecting on his pyramid-on-point personality Ed could see how The Voice was the commentary that kept him spinning and fuelled his innate restlessness. It had been the encouragement that had driven him to the edge, up mountains and into valleys, voraciously engaging in self-promotion, to win, to eat more and drink to excess, baiting and mating. It was The Voice that told him the answer was in the barrel of a wave, or down the barrel of a gun. Or in a hole in one. It demanded greatness and then criticised it. Always wanting more or different.

Of course The Voice could be subtle too, and coercive, seductive or casual. It knew how to work him; his likes and dislikes, tendencies and tipping points. It was The Voice that had said he needed to leave his cliff-top retreat and go to the wedding. Now it was telling him he needed to get the hell out.

Meditation was tough because it meant hearing The Voice *without re-action* which in Ed's experience often demanded more skill and courage than the action it commanded. Climbing a cliff or jumping off a bridge or kayaking down a waterfall was easy compared to sitting on a cushion in a room quietly by himself.

Hearing The Voice, without acting, was equivalent to slaying the dragon.

And it was the first step in having his pyramid rest on its base.

And Ed was winning. By choosing stillness instead of excitement, and simplicity rather than intensity – like now, here in the gazebo – he could land, settle and rest, and open up a dialogue with his true self.

"Ah!"

He began to see how these months of meditation and quietude and self-reflection on the cliff-top had been a process of undoing the mechanism of delusion. Of releasing this high maintenance, false sense-of-self. Of dropping pretence, allowing the pyramid to settle on it's base, to find the ground of his true being.

Most of all, discovering there is nowhere to fall.

He could clearly remember the day, the moment, when he first allowed himself to drop all the stuff that normally holds his attention, to exclude everything that wasn't *here*. And wasn't *now*.

What a relief!

Without his attention it ceased to exist.

At that moment he was feeling so much devotion for the cabin and everything it had given him.

Today at the wedding, under pressure, he had reverted to habit. In the language of the pyramid example he had been flipped back onto a point – was sent into a spin – automatically feeling the need to defend, justify and fill the space.

But all was not lost, even during his verbal stampede at dinner there was a quality of awareness – he had found the courage to enter and blend with everything that was going on, inside and out. And missed dessert to take a time-out, to lean back against a tall tree and look up into the branches and take some breaths. Instead of being consumed by everything that wasn't happening, he had allowed himself to be fully distracted by the present moment, senses open and alive, aware of it all, processing none of it. This was progress.

And now he had an image, a measure. The pyramid described his options; there was the habitual, forced, false version standing on point. Or the pyramid resting on its base representing a natural way of being, which was like discovering an inner refuge. Just knowing it was there, free and available, was a comfort and gave him confidence. There was something he could do, a place within himself he could go. Or come back to.

Coming to this wedding really was feeding himself to the lions. And being spat out was good for his pride. He laughed at himself, with himself.

He'd spent years clocking up air-miles looking for a special something, boggled by the scope and range of possible experience, trying to cover that ground, never accepting it's impossible to go everywhere and do it all.

Looking outside of himself he could always dream of something better, of a freedom greater than the one he already had – the only limit was his imagination.

Now he understood that within himself was a freedom beyond even his imagination.

How could he have missed it? Why had he found it necessary to tick so many boxes and strike through so many options before coming to such an obvious and clear conclusion?

It's time for another excuse.

Each year Ed's family in Wales received a Christmas card stuffed with polaroids from The Australian Cousins.

Surfing sets at Bondi and barbeques on the beach, water skiing on azure water and snow skiing in waist deep powder, sailing yachts, shark fishing, diving on The Great Barrier Reef, driving their own jeep into the outback to wrestle with crocodiles, leaping out of aeroplanes, marathons, iron-man triathlons, ultra-distance multi-discipline extreme pursuit events. And all of it under an infinitely perfect blue sky.

The festive lights blinked, cold rain fell out of the darkness and hammered at the window as teen-aged Ed picked at the finger nails of his pale hands, poring over photographs of his chestnut coloured cousins.

Ed had been distracted by the Bahamas and bits of Asia and America – now he was ready for the real thing, the ultimate prize, the god realm.

Ed was ready for Australia.

hot desert

doors

They were having a farewell drink in The Maya Bar in Kathmandu, Nepal. It was happy hour but Barry was concerned. He looked across the table at Tracy with his mohawk, ink and piercings, and at Ed with his bandana, dreadlocks and barefeet on the table. He felt the need to give them some advice. After all he was their boss.

"Lads, I'm Australian, I love Australia, Australians are cool, but you need to take it handy going through Sydney immigration, they can be more than shitty, worse than Heathrow. If they don't like the way you look, or sound, or smell, they'll send you right back on the next flight – at your expense, and that's expensive!"

"It's okay, Baz, we know how to behave," said Ed. Tracy wasn't listening.

"Which airline are you flying with?" asked Barry

"Singapore."

"Oh no, that's dangerous."

"What? No, they have a great safety record."

"Yeah safety as in take-off and landing. I'm talking about the complimentary drink and cigs. "

"Ooo, see what you mean…"

"Ooo, see what you mean…" added Tracy. He was listening now.

Ed was woken up by a woman, she was leaning over him smiling. It was the wife of the Singapore Airlines pilot, the one he had sat next to on the plane.

Ed's mind raced to bring himself up to date.

She was fully clothed.

So was he.

He was lying on the floor.

"I think you two will enjoy Australia." she said and walked off, her high heels clicking, gold accessories jangling.

Tracy was next to Ed, folded over his back-pack, still asleep. On the other side of the glass was a line of taxis. Above him there was a large neon sign saying ARRIVALS.

They were in Australia.

Winter was coming so after hanging out in Sydney for a while, they decided to go north to Brisbane for a bit of warmth and sunshine.

Ah, that's better!

They were drinking coffee and eating croissants in a beach café. Ed was studying the job ads "Opportunity for young people to earn good money and travel Australia…"

"Fuck off," said Tracy losing some crumbs in the process. He licked a finger and chased them around the table and back into his mouth, then snatched the paper off Ed, straightened it, and turned it the right way up.

"Opportunity for young people to earn good money and travel Australia," he repeated. "Well, you'd have to be a right twat to fall for that."

"I'm phoning."

"You're a twat."

When Ed got back his coffee cup was empty. Tracy had switched them. Ed pretended not to notice, he didn't want to start a fight, he wanted to share the news.

"You'll never believe it!"

"You're a twat?"

"We've got interviews!"

"You *are* a twat."

The lads cycled into town and waited outside a pseudo-swanky office building until they stopped sweating. Once inside they took the lift to the top floor and were ushered into a large conference room. They meandered through a sea of fresh young faces to the refreshments table at the back where they drank tea and ate biscuits until three suits came in, wished everybody a Good Morning, thanked them for attending, and then described the perfect job – without saying what it actually was. It sounded something like a Sales Representative for a company that produced educational packages. Tracy was fidgeting, he'd been duped like this once before and had been nervous about employment ever since.

They were invited to mingle and help themselves to refreshments while their names were called to have a one-on-one with the company representatives at the front of the room. When it was Tracy's turn he took his mug of tea and a plate of biscuits with him.

After that they were all thanked once more and requested to ring the number on the leaflet after three that afternoon to find out if they had got the job.

Ed put the phone down very slowly. "You'll never believe it!"

"We got the job."

"That's right. Scorio! How cool is that?"

"Scrambles, did you happen to notice the state on the other applicants; pin heads and losers. Of course we got the job."

"You know some people say they never get a break. Maybe it's just because when the luck comes they look the other way."

"Shut up. You *are* a twat and now you are making it worse."

Tracy agreed to attend the two-day induction course only because meals were provided and they received an allowance toward their accommodation. And he was sure that Cute Caroline in the business suit (with whom he had shared his biscuits at the interview) would also be one of the successful applicants.

So the boys spent the next two days wearing clean t-shirts sitting in meeting rooms being trained in their new job. They learned that their new employers produced and sold books.

"You don't mean encyclopedias do you?"

"No, this is a complete educational package for children from pre-school to university age."

Ed was wondering what the hell he'd got them into, but it was Tracy's turn to be enthusiastic. He was turning into the star pupil, especially for the module where you learn all the tricks you would ever need to get yourself invited into a stranger's house. And the session about knowing how someone will answer a question before you even ask it.

At the end of the training they were told which teams they would be joining; Tracy's team was based back in Adelaide. Ed was doing his head in, his neck was already sunburned and the bus ticket was paid for – so why not?

Ed was heading south too, to Melbourne. He was less and less inspired and spent most of the long bus journey trying to encourage himself by identifying some positives.

He came up with two:

First, how would he ever know if he never tried it? The sales training was all hype and dynamism – can you really make someone smile by putting your arms up in the air? And knowing how someone will answer a question before you even ask it would be fun to try.

That was all Positive Number One.

Number Two was Dean Moriarty. Dean Moriarty was the hero of Jack Kerouac's masterpiece *On The Road*. The Moriarty character is based on the real-life Neal Cassady who once did a brief spell of Encyclopedia selling. So Ed was viewing this adventure as some kind of rite of passage into beat culture and the Hall of Hip Fame.

Maybe related to that, or perhaps it was a third point all on it's own, was when during the training one of the new recruits had asked a question, something about articles which were appearing in scientific journals regarding a "world wide web library" currently under development which would be an almost limitless information resource that anyone with a home computer could "dial in to". *And* it would be free! It sounded so mad that the alpha-female facilitator leading the session quickly had the lad who asked the question blushing hard. She even said, *Too much knowledge is a dangerous thing,* which in the context seemed a little harsh – and strange. But, thought Ed, if Blushing Geek Boy is on to something, he better dig this Encyclopedia Selling experience now because very soon it could all be history.

Of course, a fourth plus point was the prospect of earning lots of money very quickly so he could continue on his worldwide search for whatever it was he was looking for.

So, sitting on the Melbourne-bound bus, as the needle swung from Red Ridiculous into Green Why Not? he relaxed enough to fall asleep. Hopefully when he woke up his hangover would be history.

After Ed and Tracy heard the news that they had got the jobs they had to go out and celebrate – those were rules.

Tracy proudly produced a scrap of paper with Cute Caroline's number on it.

"This was hard-won, I can tell you."

He made the call.

"She's got a friend. They'll meet us in the bar down the street."

The bar was like a gymnasium. Vinyl floor, strip lighting, a boxing match was being shown on a huge screen on the far wall. Caroline and Tina arrived on time. They were wearing tracksuits.

There were no other women in the bar except the three barmaids who were in a huddle, looking at a clock, discussing the time. It was exactly eight o'clock. They disappeared through a door at the back of the bar. A minute later they came back. Topless. Naked from the waist up.

The Tracksuit Twins didn't seem phased. Tracy offered to go to the bar, leaving Ed at the table with The Twins. Ed pretended to watch the boxing and repeated a mantra – *everything's cool, everything's cool.*

Usually pubs had low ceilings and flagstone floors with fires blazing, or were wooden cabins with rickety wooden benches, shutters on the windows and skis nailed to the walls. They were dark and smoky, places where men and fully dressed women could hide and drink, and hide in the drink. This was different.

Ed had the feeling someone was standing behind him. He turned his head and the end of his nose brushed a breast.

"Can I get you folks a drink?" asked the waitress.

"You can, yes you can, we will, I'm, we'll all have four beers please," said Ed without blinking.

Ed's barmaid sashayed off in the direction of the bar, sidestepping Tracy who was on his way back to the table carrying a pitcher and four glasses.

Ed had a bout of 'sewing machine leg' – under the table his right knee was vibrating up and down in a blur. They clinked glasses and drank.

"Did you two go to university?" asked Cute Caroline.

Ed had just taken a big swig of fizzy ozzy lager so Tracy fielded the question.

"He did," said Tracy pointing across the table.

"What's the first day like?"

Ed sneezed a mouthful of fizzy ozzy lager over the table – just as the bare-chested barmaid returned and dangled sixteen more beers…

Caroline and Tina had just left school, Caroline had gone for the interview and completed the two-day training just for a bit of real-world practice.

"You'd have to be desperate to take a job like that," she said.

"Yeah, well, we just wanted the bus tickets south."

At 10.00pm Caroline called her mother and they were picked up.

Ed and Tracy were discombobulated. They called a taxi and went into town where they became an even-longer-word meaning trashed.

The next day, on their way to the bus station, Ed bought two collared shirts and a pair of slacks in a charity shop. He and Tracy were too hungover to say goodbye. They just wandered in different directions and got on different buses.

More than twenty four hours later Ed unloaded his bag and bike from the belly of the bus in Melbourne. He'd decided to bring the bike with him rather than sell it in Brisbane because in this new job they only worked in the evenings so he could spend the days exploring.

He found a call box and dialled the number he'd been given. It was for a mobile phone. That was exciting. And disturbing. It was exciting because Ed had never called a mobile phone before, and it was disturbing because it was 11pm and the person who answered said the team were still out working – surely they should be popping the tops off a few cold ones by now.

The mobile person on the mobile telephone had told him to

get a taxi to their accommodation. The address he had been given was a caravan park. He told Taxi Driver that he'd got a job selling educational packages. Taxi Driver was sceptical and she was no wimp, she had just finished telling Ed the story of how she was the guardian of her grandson – ever since the boy saw his father kill his mother with an axe.

The key to the chalet was where they said it would be and he a took a top bunk like he was told to. By two in the morning The Team were still not back and Ed could not sleep. At 2.05am they arrived back. They switched on all the lights and made themselves vegemite-on-toast. Ed didn't know whether to get out of bed in his boxer shorts and introduce himself, or feign sleep. Forty five minutes later he still hadn't decided. They switched off the lights. That's decided then.

That was Thursday night. On Friday he got up at 10am. It was raining. Everyone else was sleeping. He put the kettle on, it was very loud.

At midday he met his new colleagues on their way to the shower. By 1pm everyone was washed and dressed and having a vegemite-on-toast breakfast at the team meeting.

There were fourteen people in the team. The boss was called Aidan, he had a twitch. His girlfriend looked like a painted wooden doll, her name was Meg, she was The Sales Guru. There were three other sellers and Ed was the newest of nine appointment makers.

This team was a well-oiled machine. They had made thirty-four sales that week, a new company record, but Aidan was sure they could make forty by Sunday evening.

"Really? You work on a Friday night *and* all the weekend?" Ed said out loud, even though it was only supposed to be a thought.

"We especially work on Friday night and the weekends," said a few of them together.

After the meeting the team broke up into pairs and threes for training; smiling in the mirror, learning the script, doing the postures.

"We warm up here, not on the turf – we don't want to waste doors."

Aidan and Meg paraded round checking everyone was fully engaged.

"If you act enthusiastic you are enthusiastic..."

The new recruits had been asked for a commitment of at least three weeks – to give it a proper go and to honour the investment the company had made in the training. This was only Day 1. Ed listened and he tried. Three weeks seemed like a very long time already.

Neal Cassady had done this.

Even though Neal Cassady had done this Ed was struggling.

On their first night new Appointment Makers shadow an experienced colleague and Ed would be shadowing Bruce. Bruce was Aidan's best Appointment Maker. Bruce was the world's best Appointment Maker. The only reason he hadn't been promoted to Sales months ago was because he was a once-in-a-generation, reincarnated-for-this-very-purpose Appointment Maker. Still, Aidan was nervous.

Head Office had no sense of timing, imagine sending down a new recruit when they were this close to history.

Aidan calmed himself, he knew Bruce always got appointments, and they always sold, Bruce will handle it...

At 5pm they all boarded the bus. It was more than an hour's drive to "the turf" they were currently working. Plenty of time for extra motivation; Aidan called out the questions, the whole mini-bus sang back the rehearsed responses.

"What beats resistance?"

"Persistence!"

"What defies defeat?"

"Determination!"

"What's it all about?"

"It's an exciting programme we're introducing to *all* the families in the area – it's nothing personal or religious and I'll keep it as brief as possible – can I come in?"

"We're not interested!"

"I understand, but we would like to talk to *as many* families as possible – I'll be very quick, do you mind if I come in?"

Then there were cadet marching songs and show tunes. Against his better judgement Ed jumped in and let the current take him.

If the mood dipped, Aidan pulled into a lay-by and made them all get out and jog around the bus. Finally they were there and the Appointment Makers were dropped one at a time. Each time someone got out there was applause and shouts of encouragement. "Yeah! Let's get out there and battle!"

One by one the bus got emptier. All the Appointment Makers had been dropped except Bruce and Ed.

Ed was stoked! They were not climbing out of a minibus, they were skydiving from 20,000 feet. He floated off down the road behind Bruce.

First Ed had to learn how to smile Bruce-style. An all-the-way-through smile that made other people smile too.

"Dude, we're out here to have fun."

Bruce covered his face with his clip-board so Ed could only see his eyes and still Ed could see the smile.

They rounded a bend. The first house, the first door-bell.

Their job was, without wasting any time, to create a situation where they were speaking to both parents, then establish that both parents could speak reasonably fluent English, that they had one or more children of school-age, and that at least one of them had a stable full-time job. If they ticked those boxes the Appointment Makers could and should schedule a Demonstration which was code for letting one of Meg's elite sales team off their lead. An Appointment Maker got paid for any sale resulting from a demonstration they had scheduled.

Between houses they jogged.

"I'm positive! I'm confident! I'm enthusiastic!" chanted Bruce and waited for Ed to repeat it.

"I am positive, I am confident, I am enthusiastic."

"Okay. Now say it like you mean it…Okay! Now louder!"

Bruce going down a street had the same effect as an ice-cream van playing it's jingle, smiling people came out to meet him.

Another house; in moments they were invited inside, they hadn't even shown any ID or said why they were calling – and yet they were sitting on a sofa in front of a tray of tea and biscuits.

"Wait a minute," said Bruce suddenly to the couple opposite them, "something's wrong, you're too happy, you don't have kids do you?" Even Bruce had let the excitement get the better of him – what a lapse! Ed was just reaching for some ginger cake when Bruce stood up and apologised – they had to leave, they had customers to meet. He bid them farewell, vaulting their hedge into the neighbours garden.

"I've got the juice! I've got the fire! I've got the burning desire!"

It seemed to Ed you could get away with murder if you were smiling.

Approaching the next house. "See the signs," Bruce said, pointing to the trampoline in the garden, booster seats in the car, and little welly boots lined up on the porch.

It was time. Ed would try the spiel. He rang the doorbell.

The answer was *No.*

Ed's apology for disturbing their evening trailed away to nothing, and turning down the path his shoulders rounded, his heart was in his heels.

"Hey, wow! No, no, no, *NO!* Always leave more enthusiastic than when you arrived. Every time. Remember, we're searching for diamonds in a rubbish heap here, and you are one step closer to the big one! It's not about hope it's about belief. Always, all the time, be the most enthusiastic person you know."

They jogged on to the next house.

"I'm alive, I'm alert and I feel great!"

"I'm alive, I'm alert and I feel great!"

At the next house Ed left Ed at the gate and skipped up the path. These parents had no children of school-age but they thanked the boys for their visit.

Bam! Bruce gave Ed a high five and a low five and another high five.

"You're getting it! It's happening!"

On Saturday morning Ed got up, had his shower, went to the meeting and tried to eat vegemite-on-toast without screwing his face up. During the afternoon training he was made to door-knock in the mirror. Smile in the mirror. Arrange appointments in the mirror. Take rejection and smile about it in the mirror.

" Do you know who are the most highly trained employees in Disneyland? The car park attendants. Do you know why? Because they are the first people you meet."

Today Ed was going to fly solo.

He was the last Appointment Maker to be dropped. Aidan called him up to the front passenger seat and illuminated a map with his torch and put two red crosses on it.

"This is where we are…this is where I pick you up." Then he inked in all the roads between the two crosses. "And these are your streets."

Aidan clapped and cheered him out the door. Ed was off up the path to the first house like he was running out of the tunnel at Wembley.

He hammed up the pommie accent, was invited inside and within a minute had ascertained their vocation, how many kids they had and what age.

"And you're free tomorrow night if my manager was to call round with a free no-obligation demonstration are you? Excellent."

He was getting into half the doors he knocked on, a great average, and after 160 houses he had two appointments, which was two more anyone had expected him to get, so he relaxed and went off the boil a bit. There was still another hour before pick-up and so he ducked into a bar near the second red X.

Aidan was on time picking him up and was picking him up first so he could diffuse any frustration and transform any disappointment before it could influence anyone else.

Ed was buzzing as he told Aidan he had made two appointments and confessed to having had a little celebration, quickly adding that the barmaid had kids but she didn't want him to demonstrate anything. He was sure this would make Aidan even pleased-er. Aidan wasn't even a little bit pleased – in fact he flipped. Apparently there was no end to success, we should always strive for more and enough is never enough!

Sunday. As usual The Team scraped itself into action for one o'clock in the afternoon. The training was frenzied – the magic forty – is it even humanly possible?

Which is when Aidan made his *nearly* final mistake. He

wanted to inspire Ed, and light the fire of insatiable desire, so he gave him the day off appointment-making. Today, as they closed in on the magic forty, Ed was going to shadow Meg. For the past two weeks Meg had converted all her appointments into sales, she was on the ultimate roll. This would be a master class. Ed knew he was expected to pop with excitement, but he didn't. Meg was watching Ed in her make-up mirror. She looked like a horror movie.

Meg and Ed's first appointment was at the home of an Indian family. They were impressed with the product. When Meg paused in her presentation they nervously asked about the price. The question was deflected, the demonstration progressed and their interest intensified into desire, which is when Meg slipped the price in. She may as well have stuck a knife in. The parents deflated. It was beyond them. They said so.

Meg described the "easy-pay scheme". That was beyond them too. They said so. They thanked Meg, and apologised to Meg, but Meg wouldn't let go. She asked them questions like *Do you want the best for your children?* and *Can you put a price on your children's education?*

All this under the gaze of their beautiful brown-eyed children who had also liked the sound of everything they had heard.

Ed asked if he could use the toilet. That seemed to break the witch's spell. The bathroom was down the end of the hall, the father led him down the hall;

"Careful not to trip over the lawn mower. We need to send it back. The garden shed is still flat-packed in plastic out the back, that's going back too."

In India he had been a lawyer. In Australia he was having to take more exams just to be an accountant. He hadn't expected that.

Meg was not sure what had just happened. Back in the van she was in shock.

She held up her mirror and applied another coat.

Next was a Lebanese family. It was a similar story. The parents wanted to give their children the best education whatever it cost but they had no money. Meg wouldn't let it go until finally the father offered to show them around his house. They went into each room. He told them what everything had cost. Each piece of furniture, the fittings. At the end of every sentence he said "It breaks your back." His wife had just lost her job and she had also racked up three speeding fines so far that month.

It breaks your back.

That evening the last Demonstrator left the last house at 1am. It was a No Sale. So they had made only two sales that day, giving a total of thirty-nine.

"All right, okay," said Aidan. "This week we still broke a company record and Jodie broke ice as a demonstrator, Bruce wrote three doubles, and Kelly-Anne did a PB on her last week!"

Kelly-Anne made a little speech. *I have learned so much, not just about other people but about myself. And you guys are such a great bunch of people…*

Very late that night, back at the caravan park Aidan took Ed aside and asked if he enjoyed seeing the selling side of things. Ed told him the truth. Aidan pitied Ed.

"If we were selling bright red sports cars do you think the answer would be 'we can't quite afford it'?"

On the first night when he arrived, after being dropped by Taxi Driver, he had wanted to run away but he had made a commitment to a three-week trial. And he doesn't give up and doesn't quit. Anything. If he started reading a book, even if it was complete rubbish, he would finish it, that was the kind of person he was. Stubborn and prideful.

So the following morning – actually it was the afternoon – and it was Monday – Ed got up as usual and did what he had promised to do. He let himself be carried along by the training; he wanted to see the good in things, and succeed. He didn't want to be wrong about this. Or anything.

He was called to Aidan's cabin where Aidan told him he would be paid for the two appointments he had made – both had sold – but if they were booked down to Annie she would win the company's prize for best Novice Appointment Maker of the Month, a ski trip to Queenstown. "Is that all right with you?"

What choice did he have? They were a team. The other teams were probably cheating too. It was the final straw though. Aidan's final mistake. There was a loud crack; it was Ed's spirit breaking.

After a brief training, everyone got into the van and they drove to the turf. Everyone except Meg. She stayed back at the caravan park. She was looking for her mojo.

The weather had turned colder. And wet. Ed faked it for a few houses. No-one was convinced. Then he met an eight-year-old boy called Brendan who cycled around with him offering entertaining and useful snips of neighbourhood gossip;

"They're on holiday, back next week. They don't have kids. Those people are dead. That woman hits her husband on the head with a frying pan. They have kids."

Ed shared a chocolate bar with Brendan.

"Is it encyclopaedias you're selling?" the boy asked.

"Yeah," said Ed

"Are they any good?"

"No," said Ed. "They are really heavy. And expensive. A better version is available in the local library – and there is a new invention on the way called the InterWeb so by the time you get to secondary school, if you have access to a computer, all this knowledge will be available to you at the click of a button, and for free."

Gusting wind blew cold rain across the street, you couldn't shelter from it. Gutters leaked, paths were slick. Brendan went home and Ed found a phone box and called Aidan's house-brick mobile phone.

"Pick me up whenever you're ready, I'll be in the bar on the corner of Tasman and Richmond."

It was 9am on Tuesday 22nd, Ed's birthday, and he was leaving. He had failed.

A small six-foot-tall birthday boy got up and quietly folded two collared shirts and a pair of slacks and left them on his bunk. He unlocked his bike, strapped his bag on the back and, with a squeaky chain, pedalled downtown to the bus station.

He called the number of Tracy's relatives. Tracy had left a message with them just the previous day: *Staying in The Ocean Hostel in Adelaide until the 23rd then going to The Barossa Valley to look for fruit picking work.*

Ed bought a ticket for Adelaide and had all day on a bus to ponder; it had been a rich experience, most of the lessons were the kind best forgotten, but there were some he would hold onto.

Smiling. And relaxing. And we're searching for diamonds in a rubbish heap and you are one step closer to the big one! It's not about hope it's about belief…Always, all the time, be the most enthusiastic person you know.

orange

Ed met Tracy in Adelaide and they cycled the scenic route to a small town called Maikerie where they wasted no time looking for honest employment. The job centre was behind the gas station. Actually it was a noticeboard in the estate agent's office which was also where you paid for your petrol.

An elderly lady sat near the noticeboard, knitting, ready to answer any queries.

Did it ever get cold enough around here to wear a woollen anything?

This day it was fairly straight forward. There were four jobs displayed:

Welder, experience required.

Engineering apprentice.

Mandarin pickers (2).

Ten minutes later they were mandarin pickers and decided to go into town to celebrate. Town was one street built on a very steep hill. If any shopping fell out of your bag at the top of town you would never see it again. There were shops of every kind including, half way up the hill, the most excellent Maikerie Bakery. On leaving, as with all the other shops, it was necessary to take a moment to prepare for the incline of the pavement.

A clever person would park at the bottom, walk to the top, and fill their bag on the way down. But a really clever person would drive to the air-conditioned out-of-town mall.

The lads were looking for somewhere to celebrate the beginning of their mandarin-picking career and after ascending the street on the left side and descending on the right side opted to invest their beer tokens in the Maikerie Hotel.

This was for four reasons. It was at the bottom of the hill. They were at the bottom of the hill. It was hot. There was no alternative.

The most economical option was to buy two litre-pitchers of beer. They ordered one each. "You want glasses with those boys?"

Tracy's Encyclopedia Selling Career story was quite different. He had joined a sales team of four people, the boss was on anti-depressants and they lived in spare rooms in her house, sleeping in bunk beds. Tracy had stayed for a night, ate breakfast and left.

"That's it?"

"Yep."

They had only just ordered their latest pitchers when someone burst into the bar and shouted over the music and all the other shouting: "They are about to make the draw in the Workingmen's Club!"

He might as well have said, "There's gold in them thar hills!"

There was silence except for the jukebox music as everyone necked their beers, and any other beer that needed necking, and headed for the door.

Even the barman stubbed out his cigarette, opened a cigar tin next to the till and retrieved three yellow tickets...

"Well," said Ed, "Rome wasn't built in a day."

"I think you mean 'When in Rome…"

"I am, I mean I do…"

On the way out the door they learned that the Workingmen's Club was next to the footie pitch which, they were relieved to find out, was also at the bottom of the hill.

"The draw" was an annual event and, in this recession-hit town, everyone wanted a chance at pocketing the $900.

At the door Ed and Tracy each bought a few tickets.

"This'd be *so* cool. We could resign tomorrow without having done any work!"

"Yeaaahh! We've only just arrived and we'll be leaving with a heap of cash *and* have created two jobs. It feels good to do good."

The first step in making the draw was allowing everyone enough time to get a drink. This gave the lads an opportunity to savour the atmosphere. Which was intense. An enormous man, sweating under a straw hat, was rocking back and forth by the bar.

"That's Big James," said a local who followed their stares and guessed their question, "he badly wants to win this." The Club was full of locals who had banked, literally, on winning the jackpot.

The two tourists were starting to regret buying tickets.

It was taking forever for them to get organised, Big James was heckling and Mary-Sue had to be restrained by her daughters, and all the time Ed and Tracy were sure that one of them was going to win and they were both going to end up in hospital, and they'd probably have to crawl there, and it was probably at the top of the hill.

"Let's run for it!" They turned but there was no way out. Everyone was wearing vests or sleeveless tops and there was hotskin in every direction…writhing drink-fuelled humanity...

"And the winner is…"

Please no

Oh Shiiiiiiittt!

Sweet Jesus! It wasn't them.

It wasn't clear who had won, they were obviously keeping a low profile while Big James and Mary Sue and half the rest of the town took offence that some other bastard was going to walk off with their money.

It was another half an hour before the MC had the courage to make the draw for the second prize – a meat tray.

"Skip Calloway."

"Na facking way mate, Skip got it last year!"

Which set off a second round of fighting…

It had been a busy day and the lads had forgotten to arrange any overnight accommodation. They got cornered by Rod, the town's carpenter. She offered them a bed for the night but they made their excuses – *we have to go to the top of the hill* – and she didn't follow them.

They were woken up by a man dressed in a shirt and tie who was waiting for the bus. A commuter.

"Shit, we've got jobs too!"

They cycled for half-an-hour to the mandarin orchard, and spent six hours with hang-overs scrabbling around in the bushes without so much as a sniff of a cup of tea. They over-dosed on mandarins instead.

The boss said every time they filled the trailer they would be paid $200. The trailer was big, towed by a museum-piece tractor which Tracy referred to as *the company vehicle*. Although they didn't get to drive it. Nobody did. There was no need. Mandarin picking is a slow and tedious business, you have to snip them from the tree with shears, it's fiddley, needs both hands. The tractor didn't move but they could swear that the trailer was growing, so they targeted the biggest fruit to fill it quicker. One of the old hands came round to see how they were getting on.

"We're strip picking," he told them.

"Oh, are we? Okay," said Ed.

"No. *We* are strip picking. You two feckwits are just picking the easiest, biggest fruit to fill the trailer quicker. Start again from the end and strip pick."

They were sent back to the end of the row to pick all the fruit – big'n'small, inside'n'outside – which meant getting twigs in their hair and face and ears.

Cycling home they both got punctures.

The nice lady at the employment board said that if they wanted budget accommodation they could try Dessie at the camp site.

"No new jobs in, I s'pose?..."

She looked at the empty board and then back at them and shook her head sadly.

The "camp site" was a brick outhouse and a caravan in a field.

The caravan was available. That was the first bit of good news all day.

Not long before the end of the second day they finished their first trailer of mandarins. Looking back at the strip-picked trees there was a tidiness to the scene they were leaving behind, and a sense of accomplishment they could take with them. The trees had been respected not exploited. That said, mandarin picking was a highway to nowhere.

"This is not viable. You can drink it quicker than you can earn it."

They went home via the employment board which was empty.

Nice Lady was knitting away at her desk. "We've got lots of jobs today. I just haven't had a chance to post them yet." She gave them a sweet smile and paused – either she was taking the piss or having one.

"…orange picking!" she said finally.

Oh Mercy! The only people who would be grateful at the opportunity to pick oranges were mandarin pickers. Oranges are as big as footballs and you can yank 'em off the tree – they'd have that trailer full in no time.

New job meant there was a celebration to plan. They liked to learn from their mistakes and mandarin picking with a hangover had been a nightmare, so they let Nice Lady know they could start the day after tomorrow – and asked if there were any bars other than the Maikerie Hotel.

"Not in Maikerie."

They called Mandarin Boss. He was a nice guy. He said he was sorry to let them go, said they were good pickers, said he'd save them the trouble of coming out to the farm – he'd bring their wages round to Dessie's camp site.

Funny how good it feels to receive a sincere compliment. Sometimes it doesn't matter who from or what for. You may have spent two hot days scrabbling around with your head stuck in a spiky tree earning a pittance, but if someone says a genuine *thank you*, well you'd nearly just turn around and do it all again.

Especially if you know you are not going to.

The Maikerie Hotel was dead. Nice Lady was serving behind the bar, surely that's illegal having all the jobs yourself? She didn't seem to recognise them dressed up for the evening – with wet hair and fresh vests – in fact it wasn't her, the wheeze on this one was different. In that case she would not know they had just got jobs picking oranges, so they told her.

"Yeah," she gasped, "it's great news about the boat…" hand on hip, big breath, reaching for the second pitcher, "…there's a real buzz around the town."

At that moment they heard someone drop a plate in the kitchen which was at the other end of the building.

They went to bed sober and woke up early. Only then it dawned on them…

They were in Maikerie.

And they had the day off.

In Maikerie.

The plan had been to miss most of the day in bed with a hangover – not have a day doing nothing. They read books, played cards, swapped books.

They borrowed the radio from the shelf above the top-load

washing machine in the brick outhouse and took it in turns to try to locate a signal other than the local radio station.

During a Buy and Sell slot one caller said they were looking to buy guinea pigs, or rats, lots of them. This got the DJ interested. "Oh yeah, are you going to tell the listeners what you got going on down there?"

"I've got a six-foot python that needs feeding that's what I got going on."

This was followed by more ads.

Next was an interview with a professor from Sydney who was explaining how they had just discovered a new pain killer that was derived from the Ecuadorian tree frog.

The DJ was buzzing; "Yeah, yeah, sound's great. Isn't that fascinating, that a tree frog from Ecuador could help relieve the pain of millions of people…"

"That's right," said the professor, justly proud, "currently we are only at the testing stage. We have been injecting rats and then sitting them on a hot plate. Of course some jumped in the air, but others were able to stay there for quite some time."

Ed expected the DJ to make a joke,

"Hey, Prof, not sure how reliable that experiment is though, I mean how do you know they are jumping because of the hot plate? I mean if you injected me with Ecuadorian tree frog extract I reckon it would put a spring in my step... hah hah, blah blah...."

But the DJ seemed distracted.

"Right, right. Interesting. Thank you. Okay listeners, we've got some music here to play, but Professor please stay on the line, I want to put you in touch with someone…"

Of course! DJ man was trying to make a buck on the side. The professor's semi-sautéed vermin would make a tasty meal for a six-foot snake.

The day passed. Slowly. Maybe because the sky is bigger in Australia it takes the sun longer to go from one side to the other?

That night it rained. And it was cool.

In the morning the lads felt some purpose, excitement and enthusiasm about starting their new job which, in the circumstances, they felt was excusable.

Dessie stopped them at the gate, said they should call the orange farm first, pointing to the call box. He walked over with them.

Ed put the phone down. And shut his mouth slowly. And began pushing his bike in the direction of the caravan.

"Yep," said Dessie to Tracy, "I figured…too wet and too cold to pick oranges. That's a bitch…what with the boat being on it's way'n'all."

They had *another* day off in Maikerie.

The books were read, three of the playing cards were missing, more radio was not an option.

"I'd rather be alone with the voices in my head than listen to any more of that bullshit," said Tracy, slamming the door behind him.

Ed was all alone. "Bastard. I was going to go outside."

That night it was again wet. And cold.

In the morning the boys sneaked out the gate without Dessie seeing them and went up to the orange farm anyway.

They met the Orange Farmer on the steps of his house, he was scratching his palms and close to tears. The vista was huge and it was full of orange trees bearing ripe fruit.

"See all this…I am third generation but it was never like it is now, not for my father and not for his father. We have to supply oranges when the supermarket wants oranges, not before, not after. When the supermarket gives the nod, they send the boat. We have to get it picked and packed and to the port because if we miss the boat, well, y'know, we've missed the boat. Then the oranges fall off the trees and rot on the ground. But now, now when it looks like it may nearly be possible, we get *this* weather. These days being good at your job is not good enough. You have to be lucky just to survive. Even then I'm not sure it's possible. I gave up trying to control it years ago, but now I think I have to give up altogether."

Wow. It doesn't matter how talented and enthusiastic an Orange Farmer he was, he was only human, one human, at the end of an impossibly complex chain of interdependence that did not have his best interests at heart. He was the one that supplied the oranges but if he couldn't do it in the right way at the right time then they would just find someone else. He knew it and so did they. It was a blue-print for a miserable life. Ed and Tracy pedalled back to their caravan in shock.

Ed was somewhere between exploding with anger, imploding with compassion and the relief of knowing none of it was his problem. For the first time in his life, and just for a moment, he was high in the sky looking down on the human species busying itself with trivial occupation.

That evening the lads couldn't resist the temptation to celebrate the fact that they did not own a farm. Or any kind of business. Or have any responsibility.

They were still in Maikerie but they felt so very lucky.

The Hotel bar was closed and the bottle shop at the top of the hill was shut. Luckily they had helped themselves to a few oranges as they left the farm. They would celebrate by having oranges and custard for tea.

"Oops. No. Out of custard powder. Want a digestive with it?"
"Aye, go on."
"We don't have any."

That night it didn't rain, the sky was clear but it wasn't cold. It would be a fine day.

They were early for work. After three days off in Maikerie the prospect of having something to do was a huge relief. That said, anybody with a beating heart would be motivated to help Orange Farmer get as many boxes of his pesky oranges loaded onto that damn boat before everybody changed their mind or a storm hit or…

They were relieved to see Orange Farmer was alive and well. In fact he was all smiles and rolled-up sleeves. Human nature is so resilient. To the point of being stupid.

At the next moment a Massey Ferguson 135 came smoking around the corner, piloted by a man with a face like a pumpkin. Sitting on one wheel arch of the tractor was a human being wearing a dress, sitting on the opposite wheel arch was a small coffin, no…it was a large hi-fi speaker.

"Here come Herb and Margaret," said Orange Farmer. "Follow them, they'll show you the ropes."

The tractor swerved violently off at a right angle and headed off down one of the rows.

Herb and Margaret had fourteen years experience. Although recently they'd had some time off too.

"Last week the Boss was round the house a few times looking for us to work. I knew it was him knocking but I didn't answer, I couldn't move with a hangover. I'd drunk a bottle of Irish Cream and a slab of beer. I was out for two days. I need the money though, I am looking to buy a horse to pull my buggy."

Margaret seemed sweet enough but she'd been diving into

orange trees drunk, half-drunk or hungover for over a decade and, well, she looked like it. She was mostly deaf and half blind.

The lads were each handed a giant kangaroo-pouch apron bag which looped over the head and tied up around the back with a front pocket big enough to carry fifty kilos of oranges at a time.

Ed strapped himself into his apron bag and climbed the ladder. The morning air was cool and fresh, the leaves and fruit glistened bright under a film of dew. From the top he could see the ends of the earth in every direction, vast and blue. The silence was even bigger.

"Herb....*Herb!*" screamed Margaret from under a tree, "Herrrrbb!...Put the feckin radio on...and loud enough for me to hear it properly."

The radio jock, who was part of the family by now, played Tasmin Archer's *Sleeping Satellite* while Ed was at the top of the ladder. Orange trees stretched to the horizon in every direction and the pristine sky arched over everything. Standing on that ladder, under that sky, Ed felt like a caveman in a cathedral.

"Not even elevenses and we've a hundred dollars already," said Ed looking at the trailer.

"Er no," said Herb, "with oranges it's hundred dollars for a full trailer."

Days passed.

Ed developed a simple technique to keep things interesting. He picked a pouch-full at ground level and unloaded it into the trailer. Then picked a pouch-full from half-way up the ladder and unloaded that. Then went to the top of the ladder for a load.

A number of times he was at the top of the ladder when the

DJ played *Sleeping Satellite* but it was never the same as that first day. How quickly marvel becomes mundane.

More days passed.

And then *The Day That Changed Things* dawned.

Over the noise of Herb's tractor radio they didn't hear Tracy shouting. Ed just happened to look up and see a pair of legs kicking wildly in the top of a tree. "What the…?"

This is how it happened;

Tracy's bag was nearly full and he had faced the familiar dilemma – *will I waddle down the ladder and empty my bag now, or try and fit another one in.*

He was standing on the top rung, letting his very full bag of juicy fruit rest on the top of the ladder, so the ladder was taking most of the weight, as you do, when he saw one very big orange out to the right, it was just beyond his finger tips, he leaned out only a tiny bit more, his back straining and the ladder creaking...

Suddenly the bag swung like a pendulum and gravity sucked the half-a-hundredweight of citrus strapped around his neck towards the earth's core.

But Tracy didn't hit the ground, he became wedged upside down in the 'V' of a branch, pinned there by the weight of his harvest. He kicked his legs and shouted before giving up hope of being rescued and decided to try to bounce-and-wriggle himself free.

It worked. The branch snapped and he slapped into the ground, landing in several season's worth of rotting fruit. His full bag of freshly picked fruit landed on top of him.

Herb had dived in and unstrapped the bag so Tracy could crawl out into the open. Which is when Ed arrived, to find Tracy shakily getting to his feet with a crooked smile and one very big orange in his right hand.

Now Tracy was standing by the trailer next to Herb and Margaret, waiting for the blood to return to his feet. Herb was sharing a hip flask with him, Margaret crushed a can of cider in her fist and looped it into the trailer.

Ed looked at the three of them; it was like the Tim Burton movie where all the scarecrows come to life.

That evening Dessie knocked on the caravan door. It was three weeks after Ed's birthday and some letters and a parcel had been forwarded on from various places.

This was too much for Tracy who got up and left. An hour later he was back with five litres of Lambrusco, a slab of beer and a sack of crisps.

He must have walked to the bottle shop at the top of the hill for that. And carried it all the way back. He was obviously serious about getting slammed. Ed put away the letters and asked if he could join him.

The beer and crisps were gone, only the wine to go. Tracy was staring at the line of odd-looking oranges lined up on the shelf – because in real life oranges are not all orange or round-shaped as supermarkets would like us to believe. They come in many colours or look like strange faces or have arms and legs. And genitals of course.

Numerous times and using a variety of methods they had attempted to calculate how many oranges they had picked. It always came out at a different amount, the latest estimate was eighteen bins which was approximately twenty tonnes. Then the pen packed up and no-one can do sums like that in their head. Especially when they'd drunk a slab of beer and several litres of Lambrusco.

"So…," said Ed

"I don't like your tone, Scrambles. I'm relaxed, enjoying meself, don't spoil it."

"Oh, okay."

"So? What were you going to say."

"No. nothing. It can wait. Or maybe dropped altogether. You're relaxed and…"

"It's too late. Just say it."

"Well I was just thinking about your mishap today. How in many ways, I mean, I don't know, climbing the ladder looking for the juicy fruit, burdening ourselves, never satisfied, in a state of imbalance, over-reaching, only to be brought crashing back to earth. I just think maybe it's an analogy for modern society."

"I fell off a fuckin ladder Scrambles, okay. Not *everything* has to have cosmological significance. Why do you always have to look for some meta-mystical message? Please do not answer that."

Ed itched his scratched-up forearms in silence for a minute, and took a large swig of Lambrusco. "I've picked my last orange," he said.

It took a moment for his mind to catch up with his mouth, which is when he smiled.

Ed's mother had cousins in Perth which was three thousand kilometres away. The other side of The Nullarbor Plain, which is a desert. They decided to hitch.

cool pool

Ed called his mother's cousin.

"Hi, yeah, we're in Perth, no, really, oh, oh, so you didn't get our postcard? Oh, sorry. Yeah, we're in The Pirates Hostel on Melbourne Street, uh – huh, tomorrow, ten o'clock. Great, great. Yeah, thanks. Bye. Yeah, bye."

Next they cooked a massive pot of spaghetti pesto and shared it with some other guests who invited them to a party.

"Oh, sorry, no can do. Got a family re-union thing going on tomorrow. Too risky. Oh, it's just down the street is it, only walking distance? Oh , well , maybe we could come down for one and just wander back up when we're done. Okay. Cool."

The party was in an upstairs bar and Lenny Kravitz was playing live. It was someone's birthday and they were buying the drinks for anyone with dreadlocks or a mohican.

"Why the feck did you call your grandparents to come and pick us up today of all days?"

"Look, it's my mother's cousin, and yes, now, obviously it was clearly a stupid idea but last night it was not a stupid idea, last night was a stupid idea...."

"Shut up."

At ten past ten they were on the pavement wearing dark glasses. A patrol car slowed down as it drove up the street.

At twenty past ten a car pulled over. The driver was wearing dark glasses. It was Ed's mother's cousin who was Ed's mother's age. His name was Noel.

"Sorry I'm late, it's only a short drive to the house."

Conversation was difficult.

"Anita's out the back," Noel said when they got to the house.

It was still the morning but Anita was sitting in the shade and wearing dark glasses.

"Hi guys! Nice to meet you. Sorry Noel was late, we overslept. Would you like tea?" She was pointing to the pot. "Or something stronger?"

She flipped the lid off a cool box loaded with long-neck beer bottles sitting in ice.

"Noel and I are going to pop the top off a couple of cold ones. No sense in pretending, we went out last night and it all got a bit out of hand. Shambolic really."

And that was it. Ed and Tracy and Noel and Anita were friends already.

Ed's mother's other cousin, Noel's sister, was visiting family in England. Her place was a few minutes walk away and she sent a message inviting the boys to please use her house, and her car, and her swimming pool.

The house was five minutes drive from the beach; they bought surfboards and spent three happy months in Perth.

They got jobs as raft guides on the Murray River, even though Tracy had never sat in a raft before.

"I'm not sure about this," Ed had said

"Relax. How hard can it be?" Tracy replied.

An hour later Ed heard a rapping on the back door. Tracy was standing there with a cricket bat and a rubber ring under one arm and a slab of beer under the other.

He nodded in the direction of the swimming pool.

"C'mon, you're going to teach me rafting."

Later that afternoon a taxi pulled up outside. Noel and Anita fell out. They had been crewing in yacht race. Noel had convinced the skipper to make a false start and as the ocean marker buoy *hoved into focus* (that's how Noel described it), the fleet overtook them so they cheated again, turned for home, got back to the club house first and bagged the best table for the barbecue. They were so pleased with themselves.

Anita looked at the empty slab of beer.

"Well boys, where are your manners?" she said tugging at Tracy's mohican. She treated Tracy like a poodle and somehow got away with it.

"We'll just have to arrive at the party early then," said Noel.

"Wha?"

"Yes. This evening we got you invited to a house-warming party, kids of some friends of ours, let's call a cab."

"Thanks, but we can't go out tonight. We've got our first day on the river tomorrow and Tracy..."

"C'mon boys, it's Friday, stop excusing yourselves," chimed Anita all bright and breezy despite not being able to stand up without support.

The next morning Ed opened his bedroom curtains. It was very bright. Anita and Noel were standing there.

Ten minutes later Ed and Tracy were in the back of Noel's car being driven to the raft base. Actually they were hanging their heads out of the windows, imbibing fresh air and spitting toothpaste.

"When there was no answer at the door Noel said you were probably on your way already but I had a sneaky inkling that you may have overslept and checked the garage and saw the car. We were banging on the bedroom window for ages. Shambolic performance so far, gentlemen."

"And here we are," said Noel turning into the raft base.

"No, go around the block one more time."

But it was too late, Noel had already parked. It was time to put their game face on.

All things considered Tracy did very well making the transition from a cricket-bat paddle and rubber-ring rafting to the real thing.

They had six days off a week so they went to the beach a lot.

Everything was really very good and easy in Perth. They could have stayed much longer but it was too good and too easy and maybe they were afraid they were missing out on something better.

"If you can get him through the test he's yours," said Noel standing on his driveway next to a rusting tan coloured Datsun 180B.

It was a generous offer. The car was called Zeppie. No-one knew why.

They decided to drive Zeppie back to Sydney but clockwise, via Central Australia and The Northern Territories, which is a long way and a lot of desert. Many thousands of kilometres of unsurfaced roads. It looked harmless enough on their map of Australia which was a centrefold poster from a Sunday magazine.

It was hot and Zeppie had no air conditioning and one window winder was broken so they drove with three windows open at a speed that maximised air-flow while minimising dust and sand intake, which was fourth gear and fifty six miles per hour.

The roads were straight as far as the eye could see, which was a very long way. There was very little other traffic. There was no radio reception. They had four versions of a 4 Non Blondes single on a cassette tape loop.

Tweny-five years and my life is still
trying to get up that great big hill of hope…

When they found *a town* they always stopped to have a look round, stretch the legs, stimulate their minds and study the map. Each time they were surprised that a whole day of fifty-six miles per hour was less than one inch on paper.

Each day there were some cars, a few trucks and one or two "road trains" – a truck pulling three or even four trailers sometimes more than fifty metres long. They had at least ten minutes warning of any approaching vehicles and would try to guess if it was car or truck or road train based on the size of the red-dust cloud it was generating.

As the vehicle became visible, if either one of them had made the correct dust-cloud prediction they celebrated and bragged, then it was down to business. They had to wind up the three windows and, if it was a road train approaching, whoever was driving wiped their sweaty hands on their sweaty vest and got a good grip on the wheel, aimed straight and locked their arms so, in the maelstrom of the truck-and-all-its-trailers passing, they weren't blown off the road.

One day, based on the seismic size of the dust cloud, they both unanimously predicted Road Train. They were right. Tracy was driving. As Road Train got closer it appeared to be snaking wildly. Maybe the driver was nodding off? Or had swerved to flatten a family of kangaroos? Or…? Whatever it was he was taking up the whole road.

Tracy wiped his sweaty hands on his sweaty vest, gripped the wheel, locked his arms and aimed as left as he could while still staying on the road.

With all the tension Ed forgot to shut the windows. And Tracy forgot to remind him.

The monster whooshed by and they were engulfed in sand as the wind blasted and the pressure dragged on poor Zeppie. Visibility zero. Travelling at fifty six miles per hour in a blinding cloud of choking dust. There was loud bang and it went dark.

Were they dead? Ed gagged as he tried to scream. Time slowed down. He could hear angels singing. La La Laaaaaa…

Now time raced! Tracy's head was out the window, choking and spluttering, guiding Zepp to a halt at the side of the road.

Ed looked at Tracy in the driver's seat; lines of sweat streaked his red-dust-caked face. He sneezed and spat out the window and wiped his mouth. "Holy shit!" he said, cracking his mask into a smile.

"Bottle this feeling!" shouted Ed, drumming on the dusty dashboard.

In moments like that there are no worries left. The world is a very simple place. Just being alive is enough. More than enough. It's a bloody miracle!

They got out and circled the car.

Neither of the lads were mechanics but in this case they could both diagnose the issue. Zeppie's bonnet was a double-skin of rusting metal and the inner layer was still firmly locked down over the engine as it should be, but the tan coloured outer skin – while still attached at the hinge end – had been blasted up and flattened back over the windscreen and roof, like a blindfold, or as if the top half of a bird's beak had been bent back over it's head. The surfboards seemed to be unscathed but it was difficult to tell – they were pretty beat up already.

The lads took it in turns to tap-dance the outer layer of the bonnet back into place, then retied the boards on the roof using just one strap. They used the second strap to lash down the bonnet.

A few months back, in Perth, at the Vehicle Test Centre, they had looked on through the glass as monitors blinked and beeped. Would he make it?

Some guy came over and stood shoulder to shoulder with Ed, looking at Zeppie up on the ramp and said, "Mate, I've got a gambling problem, but even I wouldn't put money on that getting a cert."

Now Zeppie was not only certified, he was decorated. In the next town they decided they would treat themselves, and the next town was only a millimetre away; they would be there in a couple of hours.

The sign said "Wisconia – population 8".

There was a ten crossed out, and a seven crossed out. Wisconia was a gas station and some caravans. All eight remaining residents must have been on holiday. Or hiding. On the verandah at the gas station they found a drinks machine, with a beer option. "Civilisation, here we are! No, please, it's my round."

That night Zeppie's headlights illuminated a *Picnic* sign. They were in the middle of a major desert, obviously the picnic sign was a hallucination, and they had both seen it, which meant they were both having the same hallucination so were equally unfit to drive. It would be prudent to stop and rest. They hadn't been prudent for a very long time. They decided to give it a go. They pulled over but didn't dare go exploring.

In the outback at night it gets really dark. Really very dark. So dark it is beyond words, beyond experience. Most people would decline the challenge of describing exactly how dark it is at night in the outback. But if you met Ed on a barstool he'd attempt an answer.

"In the outback the darkness is as complete as the space is big. There are no sounds which compounds your blindness. There are millions of bright stars but they make you feel even further from the light."

If anybody was still listening Tracy would clarify. "What he means is, for example, one night we stopped for a piss, we both jumped out and went a few paces from the car and watered the desert and turned round and couldn't see the car, or each other. For a moment it was really eerie. While Scrambles had a little panic I reasoned that, as we had got out of opposite doors, and walked in opposite directions, the car must be somewhere between the two of us, so I let him continue to fret out loud and walked towards his whimper until I banged my knee on the car.

After that we took our night-time pisses one at a time and left the lights on and the engine running."

When they stopped at the hallucinated picnic site, they unrolled their sheet sleeping bags close to Zeppie. It was tempting of course to sleep with the cool night air moving over their bare skin but the sheet was protection from the sand flies that appeared at night and liked to snack on pale humans.

There was sand in his ears, behind his eyes, in his veins. Ed sat up in the light of the rising sun. They were surrounded by red rock. He was covered in red desert. Zeppie was caked in it.

"Water?" he called to himself. "Water!" he sang to the sky. "Water!!"

A boulder unfurled and revealed itself to be human. It was Tracy.

"What?"

"Water!!!"

Tracy stood up and staggered about and saw Ed was pointing and bouncing. Ed had found water. Lot's of it. A deep pool of cool.

They bathed like billionaires. Better than billionaires to be sure. A billionaire would never know this much pleasure. For billionaires there is only "very good" and "even better". To know this magnitude of luxury and pleasure you have to travel from Extreme Shite to Shangri-la in a short space of time.

They washed their clothes and laid them out on the warm rock and lobbed a few buckets over Zeppie. He looked such a cutie sitting there with his mouth strapped shut and a beret of beat-up surf-boards. And a flip-flop glued to the accelerator peddle.

Ed went to sit on the top of a tower of rock so he could see to the edge of the world in every direction. He was in the middle of everywhere. And million miles from home. And that is how he felt. He looked into the distance trying to understand the unease that it inspired until he shivered, stood up, turned around and saw a vehicle approaching.

Half an hour later a shiny white spanking new All-Wheel Drive Overland Motor-home pulled up fifty yards away. A satellite disk on the roof did a few revolutions before finding the correct co-ordinates. Within three minutes (and without anyone getting out of the vehicle) the trailer tent was erected, a boot-load of gadgets had been deployed and there was the gentle hum of a new-age generator.

In comparison, despite being washed and fresh, Zeppie and Tracy and Ed were like items recovered from an archaeological dig. The new arrivals didn't want to compare travel notes with them. They wouldn't even answer the door. Even after the boys put their clothes back on.

"What just happened?" asked Ed. It was the first time either of them had spoken since they left The Cool Pool twenty minutes before.

"We just had ourselves a bath mate," replied Tracy in his best outback accent, "that's what just happened. Our first bath in more than a week of being in a desert. Also we nearly got tazered by some highly-strung posh-gypsy Aussies."

"Yes, true. But no, what I'm asking is, what actually just happened? Don't you think us accidentally finding water in the middle of a desert, in darkness, is like a microcosm of life?"

"What? No. Stop it!"

"Stop what?"

"We had a swim okay. Can we not just have a swim and leave it at that. Can you not, just for once, be an adult and have a normal fucking conversation?"

More silence.

Tracy had thrown the 4 Non-Blondes loop tape out of the window the day before. It had started to slur – maybe the heat, maybe sand, probably just worn out – so now it was either talking to Ed, or being in his own head.

Tracy was trapped but he'd also just had a bath. He was in a great mood. If ever there was a time he could cope with Ed-shit it was now. He just had to remember not to get sucked in, take it too seriously or apply logic.

"What then? What microcosm of life have we just experienced?"

"Well, we are driving in one of the biggest, hottest deserts in the world in a car that is held together with rope and with surfboards on the roof. Our map of Australia is the centrefold of a Sunday magazine, right? We don't know exactly where we are, or where we are going, or why. And in the middle of the night and quite by chance – or was it? – we stopped next to The Pool of Cool, the only water for hundreds of miles. It was so close but we didn't see it until the morning enlightened us. Which is when we had a swim. A really great swim. In amongst all the rock and sand we accidentally found what we were looking for, as in happiness, but yet now we are following a vague map, travelling in the opposite direction back out into one of the biggest, hottest deserts in the…"

"Scrambles, please just make your point..."

"I just did!"

"Well I missed it."

"The point is that, right, actually there are two points. First, was our good fortune pure accident? Was it fate or self-determination? But second, which is the main point, how often are we that close to the answer but we fail to see it? And point 2b is, either way it's over. We are back at square one which is – in this example – driving into the hot desert going we don't know where exactly. You're probably going to say that you can't have

The Cool Pool without the hot desert, that one needs to experience a certain degree of discomfort to make the delights possible by contrast. So, is that what life's about – ninety-none per cent hassle just to get a little bit of what we want? That's not too inspiring."

"We've only got muddy water to drink and nothing to eat."

"That's right. Exactly. Now you're getting it," beamed Ed.

"No I'm not."

"Yes I think you are because the third part of my second point is, there always seems to be a push or a pull, which means even if we ever get what we want we cannot keep it. Even if we briefly get to where we want to be, we cannot stay there. It doesn't last, so we move in endless circles, caught in a loop of frustration. Why do we do that ad infinitum until we die?"

Tracy stuck his tongue and grimaced and puffed. He had the answer but if he said anything he risked getting deeper embroiled. If in doubt shut your mouth.

There was silence, except for the engine, creaking car parts and wind noise. There was no vehicle approaching, nothing else to do, he shuffled in his seat, trying to resist…Shit. Why not?

"It's fab, okay."

"I know. It's a mindfuck all right."

"No, FAB. F – A – B. What you were just talking about. Why we repeat the same mistakes over and over again. Ironically it's a survival technique, an evolutionary trait. It's why women have more than one child."

"This should be good. You on parenthood!"

"It's one of the few things a shrink said to me that I actually remember. FAB stands for *Fading Affect Bias*. Psychologists reckon that our good memories persist longer than bad memories. It helps to keep the human race happy and resilient. They say that holding onto our good memories, and leaving the bad ones behind, is a pan-cultural phenomenon and helps us to deal with unpleasant situations and retain a positive outlook on life. So we filter out the fuck-ups and then do it all over again. It's what keeps us stupid. The shrinks said I was an exception because people like me,with depression and that, we somehow manage to reverse the process. You're an exception too because you have a monkey-sized brain."

There was a pause.

"It's FEB though. F – E – B," said Ed.

"What?"

"It's FEB not FAB. *A*ffect is a verb, *E*ffect is the noun, so it'd be Fading *E-ffect* Bias."

Tracy braked and swerved. And walked towards the horizon leaving the car door open and the engine running.

Hopefully he wouldn't be too long. The sun was arcing higher and hotter, and they were low on food and only had muddy water to drink.

◆

For Ed The Cool Pool had continued to be a very rich example for a lot of what was wrong. Even that last bit where Tracy walked away was inspiring. You can try walking away from what you find difficult but (the desert is too big) eventually you have to turn and face it.

Ed was sitting in the gazebo, he was nearly ready to rejoin the wedding celebration, but first he took a moment to see if the Cool Pool episode could be applied to Pyramid Theory.

Like Cinderella's slipper!

Because even a pyramid on its point will occasionally find perfect balance. All the sand and sweat had climaxed in those few magic moments of swimming in The Cool Pool in the hot heart of the desert. Ed and Tracy's individual tweaking had perfectly blended with the infinite number of universal factors (which were beyond their control and even invisible to their senses), and at that moment it had all made sense. And felt right. Perfect even. *The pyramid was still standing on it's point, but momentarily still, in effortless equipoise.*

But this is an ever-changing world, any contentment based on external factors could not last, it never can. It will always be unstable, unreliable, unpredictable – a flash of lightning on a dark night – but it had been enough, it had confirmed that a sweet spot does exist, that it's possible. It had given him the taste and he wanted more. So he would go back into the desert until the next happy circumstance.

◆

The arrival of the air-conditioned family in the fancy motorhome meant they must be close to suburbia. And early the next day they did encounter a bitumen road and filled up with gas in a town that proudly proclaimed itself "The Asbestos Capital of Australia".

Co-incidentally Zeppie was sick. Of course he chose to spew his heroic guts when they were in a town and near a garage.

Garage Man re-lit the end of a roll up and stared into space while Ed went into way too much irrelevant detail, piecing together the sequence of events and possible cause of Zepp's difficulties.

"Start her up then, boys."

"This car is a He," said Tracy sitting in the driver's seat glaring through the windscreen at Garage Man. Tracy was not sentimental about humans or inanimate objects but Zeppie didn't fall into either category.

"Right lads. Start *Him* up then. Please."

Only then did Tracy slip his foot into the flip flop and turn the key.

Garage Man listened closely, initially full of concern, but after a few beats his demeanour lightened. He flicked his butt through the broken windscreen of a wreck without wheels. His lungs were full of smoke, so he motioned with his index finger – follow me – and led them to the corner of a barn. With the flourish of a magician he pulled an oily bed sheet off an engine – an engine that he said was from a Datsun 180B.

"This one's got the fuel pump and distributor that you need. It was going like the clappers right up until the fella rolled it. You need to find my mechanic…it won't take him long if you can get him started…there's a bar up the street, the one on the corner, maybe start looking there."

It was a miracle of modern-mechanic-medicine; Zeppie's recovery was complete, and two days later they were at Katherine Gorge National Park. Unpacking their kitchen box on a picnic table they found a real tea-bag so boiled some water.

It had been difficult getting methylated spirits for their camping stove. Pharmacies stocked it but refused to serve them, suspicious that they would drink it, or sell it on to the Aborigines in the park.

At last they found a pharmacist who would trust them, but only after they showed him the stove, and family photos they had in their wallets.

"Why don't you save yourselves a heap of trouble and get a gas stove like everyone else?"

Ceremonially passing the tea-bag through the steam, into the boiling water, watching the streaks of flavour steeping through the boiling water. Waiting. Before wringing every last drop of tea-essence out of the bag. A pukka cuppa.

The world was waking up and the morning's first passengers for the tour boat were arriving at the landing stage – a slow and steady stream of pale people moving heavily under wide-brimmed hats. Carrying a lot of plastic bags.

The boat left and the scene was erased.

For a moment.

Then came the first arrivals for the next departure. The even slower moving people. "Slow up," said Mother to her brood spread out before her, "you'll get all hot and bothered."

They dropped their belongings in the queue only to discover "someone" had left the camera film in the car.

Dad and one son trotted off to fetch it. After a while, when they had been gone too long, Mother dispatched two daughters. The family regrouped, sweaty and exhausted, just in time to see the gate close and boat number two pull into mid-stream.

The first hire canoes rounded the bend and a sight-seeing helicopter flew low above the river. It was time to move on. The used tea-bag was dry again so they tossed it into the kitchen box, packed up and set off.

A year after Ed left Australia he got a postcard from Zeppie, whose new owners were working in a ski resort.

cold desert

morning after

Tracy coughed, his body convulsing and arcing off the mattress. He called it *airing the duvet*. He fumbled through the trash on his bedside table feeling for an open pack of Marlborough Reds, couldn't find one (probably finished it during the night) so reached under the bed for a fresh pack. Eyes still closed, he deftly removes the cellophane from the box and discards the silver tab, ejects a cigarette, lights it and exhales the first breath since the coughing fit.

It was the same every morning.

"Make the tea, Scrambles." And soon after that he'd open his eyes.

Ed was already in their en suite bathroom cubicle filling the kettle.

"Ah, man, what happened to my belly-button fluff collection?"

"I had a sneezing fit in there last night, it got scattered."

"And I suppose it was an accident just like the last time..."

While the kettle was boiling Ed selected two of the cleaner looking mugs that littered the room, put an authentic imported Welsh tea-bag in each, sugar for Tracy, then poured the hot water on top. Next he brought the milk in off the window sill. It was frozen again. He knocked the carton on the desk and put a few shards in each mug, stirred and squeezed the bags, placed them on The Teabag Tower – it was the tallest it had ever been – that was growing out of a chipped mug on the corner of the desk. Ed took a sip of the steaming brew and breathed his first breath since the kettle had boiled.

The lads were a few years older now and had found jobs in a ski resort in Austria. They shared a room which had two narrow beds, two desks, one chair, a window and a door. It wasn't big enough to swing a cat. Tracy had proved it – not with a real cat, he couldn't catch one – but using Ed's pillow.

You couldn't swing a cat but if you stood on the bed you could *wind* a cat, or a pillow, which proved they lived in a room that was higher than it was wide.

On Tracy's desk was an oversized TV wired into his Playstation. On Ed's desk was his library of dog-eared books, a typewriter, tabasco sauce, a tin of new tea bags, the tower of used ones and the kettle. And the chopping board, a bread knife covered in pizza bits and everything else that wasn't on the floor.

Their room was small but it served it's purpose just about okay until, that is, they had visitors, which was often because they lived in a ski resort and most of their friends were penniless adrenalin freaks.

Ed got showered, dressed and pulled on his boots. There was something in his right shoe.

"Ha!" said Tracy.

"Ha what?"

"Ha, you put on your boot without checking for beer bottle tops. You have to buy the next case of beer."

"What?"

"It's a new game. It's called *Scorpion*."

"What happened to the old game of taking it in turns to buy beer?"

"That didn't work, we always forgot who bought the last one."

"Did we?"

Usually Ed walked up to work a bit earlier and alone. It suited him and Tracy preferred it too. This morning they were both ready at the same time so set off together. Franc passed them in his van, Tracy waved.

"I'm surprised to see you wave at Franc after last night."

"I wasn't waving, it was a Nazi salute."

The day before they had had a few beers on the way home to recover from a difficult day at the office. Actually they worked in a cloakroom not an office, and the day had not been difficult, it had been just like any other day, but they went for a beer anyway.

They began in Charly's bar, drinking with Charly at his mezzanine table that overlooked the bar and dance floor. The DJ was playing *Cotton Eye Joe* which meant it must be on, or close to, ten past six. This was their fourth season but the days had already lost all definition; *week* was just a word, *month* meant nothing. Soon after Easter the season would end.

"What's this anyway, a Welcome Celebration or Going Home Party?"

"What's the difference? How many weeks is it until Easter anyway?"

"Christmas is first."

Next they moved to Sylvie's Bar where they had their own seats, at the corner of the bar and near the window onto the street. Whenever passers-by put their faces up to the window, to see if they liked the look of the place, Tracy stuck his chin out at them. This scared most people but attracted others. Rich people live in a bubble created by their wealth, they treat the world like a theme park anyway, so the ink, the earrings, the studs and the hair were just things to Ooh and Aah about. Gosh.

"Which one of these two people is the most deluded?" asked Ed. "The first person spends the morning earning 50,000 schillings. And in the afternoon they spend it. The second person spends the whole day watching snowflakes falling. Who is the fool?"

Tracy had nearly finished his cigarette. He lit another one. He didn't reply. Long, bitter and twisted experience had taught him the best reaction was no reaction.

"Lesbian...*lesbian*...LESBIAN...lesbian."

Tracy was doing his Sean Connery impression, which was good, he really sounded like Sean Connery, but only when he said *lesbian.* When he was warmed up he tried a sentence using other words but it didn't work so he went back to *lesbian.*

Ed rolled his own cigarette. It was either that or peeling the label off his beer bottle or pairing and re-pairing beer mats. Which is when a middle-aged couple approached them.

"Hey, hello again, we are just arriving, are you remembering us? We are having a nice picture of you boys from last year, will you be having a drink?"

Ed was sure he had never seen these people before.

Ed and Tracy worked as cloakroom attendants in a ski boot depot. Each customer had a ticket with a number on it. In the morning the customer showed their number to the boys and handed in their street shoes and received their ski boots in return. In the afternoon they showed their number again, this time to exchange the ski boots for their street shoes.

Simple enough.

Until Tracy turned it into rocket science. Tracy decided the best way to work things would be for him to stay seated behind the desk and memorise the numbers of their five hundred ticket-holders. Then, when a customer came in he'd call out the number, Ed would run off to fetch the boots, and by the time the customer reached the desk their boots would be ready waiting.

Every time he got the number right Tracy would duck under the desk to take another drag on his cigarette – *This place smells of ski boots, no-one knows I'm smoking* – before correctly predicting the number of the next customer in the door.

He was usually right. Quite an achievement. Especially as Saturday was change-over day, so each week every number had a new customer.

Ed never got to sit at the desk and smoke because he had difficulty remembering any numbers.

Occasionally Tracy got the number wrong. *If* Tracy had got it wrong, then he'd look at the number on the ticket and call it out so Ed could go and fetch the correct pair. But, if Tracy had got it wrong, Ed would already be holding the wrong pair of boots and, because he had difficulty remembering one number for more than a few seconds, when he was told the right number he'd forget the wrong number, so he would not know the right place to put the wrong pair back, so he'd throw them on top of the pile of lost shoes in the corner. Meanwhile, the queue would be building up and it would take the rest of the day to get back on track. This was especially common in the afternoons when the boys were stoned.

Ed was sure he had never before seen the middle-aged couple who approached them in Sylvie's Bar that night. But hey, they were offering to buy them a drink, why be honest about it?

"Hey, yeah, good to see ye. How are ye. We're drinking Marzen," Ed said.

Tracy was tight lipped, his eyes narrowed, he looked like he may implode.

"E404 and E406!" he blurted.

The tourist couple looked at him amazed. They unzipped their jackets and produced their ski passes which had a sticker with the cloakroom numbers from the previous season.

"E404,"she breathed with wonderment in her eyes.

"E406," he gasped holding his head.

What a welcome! Luckily the couple didn't speak too much English so they left the boys to drink in peace.

"Tracy, you are a freak."

"Not really. That was an easy one. Their daughter was E405."

Ed disassembled a beer mat. "I wonder what it's like having a genuinely meaningful vocation. Does such a thing even exist? Our job is so *obviously* unimportant," he said.

"Speak for yourself." Tracy was looking at the holidaying couple who were celebrating at the bar with friends because the boy with a mohican from the boot cloakroom had remembered their number from last year.

The most common question they would ever be asked was *What do you do in the summer?* The answer that fascinated people most was *Nothing*. Imagine that, having a seven-month holiday every year. Raft guiding was another truthful reply that was always followed by more questions, which is why the boys only gave that answer to attractive females.

Tracy's current favourite was "I teach at Bible school." That killed it every time.

High in the corner there was a TV screen. During the day all they showed on every channel was skiing. In the evenings they showed highlights of the skiing.

In those days snowboarding was not yet a sport, it was an inconvenience that skiers were doing their best to tolerate, which is why it appealed to Tracy – he could enjoy himself *and* upset others.

So skiing was on the TV. This evening it was the highlights of the Women's World Cup Ten Kilometre Pursuit.

"Oh," said Ed, "I could enter that!"

Tracy exhaled. A long one. The kind that ended a century of boredom.

"Scrambles, it's the Ten Kilometre Pursuit not the Ten Year pursuit." After a pause so he could enjoy his own humour he added, "Let's get Sylvie to mute the commentary and crank up some sounds. What do you want?"

"I feel like harmonica blues."

"Thrash metal it is then," he said glaring out the window at a group of tourists muffled up in animal fur.

Whenever the boys asked Sylvie to put on some music they liked, she obliged by putting on some music she liked. That night it was Pink Floyd.

"Spot on," said Ed, "Yes indeed. We *are* just like two lost souls swimming in a fish bowl year after year. Travelling over the same old ground..."

"Scrambles, I wish you weren't here."

"I'm serious. How many seasons is this? Four? And each year we say we are not coming back. Yet at the end of each season we take our money, have another look at the world, get disappointed, and come back."

"I don't like the way this is all heading..."

"No, Tracy, this is not what you think. This is not more obscure amateur esoterica, this is actually about you and me. Fish in a bowl can swim, breed, obtain food with minimal effort and remain safe from predators. Right? But they are excruciatingly sensitive to the slightest perturbations. That's us. We didn't used to be like this. Our world is shrinking. For example the other night with that rock."

The example of the other night with that rock;

Ed went back to the room to find Tracy sitting at the table looking at an array of stone fragments spread out on newspaper.

"What are you doing?"

"I found these pieces on my way home. I am going to put it back together."

There was a tube of glue next to his left hand. He wasn't joking.

"Are you for real? I mean surely…" but at that moment Ed saw a fit and reached for the glue...

"It's not normal. It can't be healthy. We used to be fish of the sea, it took effort to sustain ourselves and we were subject to many threats but we were equal to it. Our life had variation. And we got stronger, more resilient. But this? I feel like I'm dead already."

"*When a fish learns about the land it's usually too late*. I think I read that on the back of a sugar sachet," interjected Tracy.

"What I'm saying is, we are not going to understand anything new about the nature of ourselves and our world by staying in the middle. We need some edge. No more subservient circles – we have to make some moves – bang our noses on the glass!"

On the opposite wall there was a carved Christ on the Cross.

"Take Jesus for example…" said Ed

"What? No! How can you possibly go from goldfish to the Godhead?"

"How? Like this. Yes. Jesus took off at fourteen years of age and must have had a wild time because when he came back from wherever it is he went he suddenly knew everything, and understood what he knew, and could talk in a thousand tongues and you know the rest, my point is by the time he was thirty he was sorted, very sorted, and we'll be thirty in a little more than three years and we are goldfish. And being here is not helping."

"Mmmm. Well…" puffed Tracy, "…taking Jesus as an example, Jesus upset some very important people and got strung up for it. In our case we often show up for work still drunk, we usually leave stoned, and whenever it snows you piss off snowboarding – sometimes for days at a time – meanwhile I'm having an on-off affair with the manager's fiancé. But we haven't even received a verbal warning. I mean, I don't know, what else we can do?"

Someone was leaving the bar; as they put on their coat the sleeve caught on Jesus' feet, the carving span on the nail so He was horizontal.

"Stunt Jesus," said Tracy, retrieving a battered Marlborough Red box from his jacket pocket. "Shit, only two left. SHIT! This is my last packet!"

He grabbed Ed's wrist to check the time.

"We'll miss the supermarket if we don't…" He sucked his beer bottle empty, snatched his smoke from the ash tray and raced out. He crashed back in, grabbed his coat and flew through the door again.

Ed caught up with Tracy on the steps of the supermarket. He had his nose up against the glass doors which were closed. And locked. Franc the Manager was dressed in his white grocer's coat, he was leering at Tracy, turning off the lights, slowly, one at a time. Tracy had taken his bobble hat off so his mohican was out and he was giving his look maximum aggression. Franc grinned back like a mad professor.

One of the reasons Tracy had got off his sofa, travelled the world and taken the job in Austria was because fags were cheaper. They were cheaper if he bought them in the supermarket. If he had to pay pub prices he might as well have stayed at home. Now Tracy would have to survive on two cigarettes until eight o'clock the next morning – not really an option – or pay bar prices.

He was still staring at Franc. He lit both his remaining cigarettes and smoked them. They glowed like fiery nostrils.

Ed was not as distressed as Tracy thought he should have been, as distressed as a good empathetic friend would be.

"You think this is not important? You think this does not effect you? You have forgotten we are out of milk!"

That was a low blow. Tracy knew it. No bedtime cup of tea, and – oh my god! – no tea in the morning!

Sylvie saw them through the window, she had their beers on the bar before they sat down. Tracy asked if he could borrow two packs of cigarettes until the morning. Sylvie was a good friend. And a businesswoman. She refused. She also refused to lend Ed a carton of milk – even when he said it was to feed a kitten. Especially then. Sylvie had heard that Tracy was looking for a pussy to carry out a bizarre experiment – she hoped it was a case of *lost in translation* but she couldn't take a chance.

"No!"

So Tracy spent a small fortune on two packs of cigarettes in Sylvie's Bar and immediately set about smoking them. Ed was still milkless.

European types hardly drink tea – and when they do it's not really tea, it's lukewarm water poured over tasteless ingredients someone found in a hedge – and they don't take milk. So the communal fridge in their hallway would be full of essentials like Thousand Island dressing and Huckleberry Jam but there would be no milk to rob.

Ed would have to resort to Plan B. He hated Plan B. He'd just have to be brave.

Sylvie gave him a slice of lemon wrapped up in a napkin.

"How the fuck is it these Englanders did win the war?" thought Sylvie as the boys left that evening.

Simple. It wasn't *these* Englanders.

holy

Christmas Eve in Wales is one of the biggest nights out of the year. In Austria it was dead. As if everyone had been resurrected already.

Christmas Eve of the first ski season had really caught the boys out. The bars were shut. And the restaurants. Even the supermarket was closed.

And the next season they thought the year before must have been an anomaly and were caught out again.

No-one could remember anything about the whole of the third season.

This was Season Four and luckily they had a nearly-full case of beer and enough tobacco, tea-bags and milk to calm any kind of panic.

Still, by 11pm they began to doubt themselves. It was Christmas Eve after all, there must be some action somewhere.

The village was dark and silent. The mercury was falling fast. The ice rink was empty. They slid up it and down it a few times. Close to home they bumped into The DeFre Brothers. There was no physical contact but Ed fell over anyway. Tracy invited them back to the room.

Ed, now fully revived, fetched beers off the window sill and Tracy put his Formula 1 racing game on the TV and, after a while, let The Brothers have a go.

As a backing track they had the Doodle-Sack-Thump-Mix tape turned up to number nine. Twenty four minutes later Tracy changed the mood; he turned the Playstation off with The Brothers in mid-race and fed a Bob Ross tape into the video machine. The late Bob Ross was an afro-haired white Californian who painted landscapes in thirty minutes, enthralling fans not only with brushwork but his enthusiasm for the subject

– which was usually enough to make you want to invest in his starter pack.

Tracy's Sean Connery impression was limited but he'd nailed Bob Ross, and he'd watched every landscape being painted enough times to be able to mute the sound and do the commentary himself. Which is what he did.

"Don't you love trees? I love trees. Trees are already in your brush…you've just got to shake 'em out…look, like this…let's do a raggedy old tree with lots of places for the animals to hide…wild and free just like God intended…I get tired of trees that are straight and tall with telephone companies out looking for them…and let's give this one a friend, everybody needs a friend…"

For Ed it was a hypnotic experience. When a Bob Ross video went into the machine he knew he had to be on his bed, preferably under the duvet, because sleep comes quick and heavy. Ed had never seen a finished painting.

Once, while Ed was in the shower, Tracy had put a Bob Ross video on unannounced. When Ed came out wrapped in a towel he sat on the edge of the table next to the open window.

He woke up on the floor, a frozen embryo, white fuzz on the TV screen and Tracy snoring.

night of the long table

"It's too cold for snow" is the kind of statement a British person would say to other British people next to a fire in a British pub. What do Brits know about snow and cold anyway? Except that it only happens once a decade.

Ed was in the Alps jogging home at five-thirty in the morning. It was freezing *and* it was snowing. This was not jogging for recreation or to be somewhere quicker, this was jogging for survival.

A nip of alcohol in cold weather can be warming but Ed had drunk a skinful, his sweat was cold, he needed to get home quickly or he'd wake up dead.

"Helluva night though," he said under his breath, smiling. Helluva night.

Ed, Tracy and most of their colleagues had gone to Geist, the neighbouring village, to meet up with ex-colleagues, neighbours and friends-of-friends in the basement bar of the Bacchus Keller. This was not just some kind of deep winter men-behaving-badly scene, the ladies were out too: ski instructors and the girls from the ticket office, from the Tourist Bureau, the Bank and Weissman Boutique – which included Petra Schneider who was the current Rose of Tyrol.

Racks of test-tubes filled with schnapps and Jagermeister, gins or poitín were passed up the line and with a mighty "Zum Wohl!" were emptied.

Ed was in the Alps jogging home. It was five-thirty in the morning, it was freezing *and* it was snowing. One side of the road was already clear of deep snow; he ran on that.

In Britain, where each county has a few toy snow ploughs, the roads would be impassable already. But in Austria every little village has at least one top-of-the range, state-of-the-art, big-boy snow plough.

The blazing lights of the Geist plough were moving back in his direction; as it came closer Ed could see the silhouette of Herr Schneider, Petra's father, in the cosy light of the space-age cab. The wheels were as tall as a tall man and the snow chains over the tyres rattled like an army of prisoners on their way to the gallows. And the diesel engine roared. Then *Boom!*

Suddenly Ed was on his back in the verge covered by icy debris.

"What the...!"

What happened there? Surely Schneider saw me? He must have swerved the plough and spewed a jet of dirty, freezing slush at me on purpose.

"What the...!"

Ed was in shock. He got to his feet and shook himself. Over his shoulder he saw Schneider was turning in the road, he was coming back.

"What thc...!"

Ahead of Ed was The Bridge. The Bridge was the border between Geist and Gefuhl. Schneider wouldn't dare cross it. Ed's soaked sleeves and trousers were stiffening in the cold. He was in worn out work boots. On an icy road. He'd never make it.

He had to. Ed started to run.

In the old days Gefuhl and Geist were poor hill-top farming villages. People were busy with the business of survival, they rarely left their farms, and very rarely would any strangers come visiting from the outside. The world was smaller and life was simpler, people did their best to love their family and neighbours, and took out all their frustration and aggression on the next village.

Gefuhl and Geist were separated by a valley. Except it wasn't really a valley, it was more of a ditch. And the bridge that crossed it was actually a culvert – easy to miss. But to make the division between the two villages genuine, to make it sound like something worth fighting for, people called it a *valley*, and referred to *The Bridge*.

This was especially true for the older generation who should have been relaxing in armchairs and smoking pipes in front of the fire, but instead were feisty old fuckers who revelled in incendiary argument and spiteful sabotage. There really is no rest for the wicked.

In the foyer of the Hotel Adler, there was a black and white photograph of a village scene which included a very young Adolf Winkler standing with his birth parents who were killed on the last day of World War II.

Adolf was adopted by a foster family in Gefuhl but he went to school in Geist – which made him mixed-race. The prejudice he faced on a daily basis made him strong; he became a Tyrolean downhill skiing champion and could have represented Austria in the Olympics. He wanted to. But there was something else he wanted more. Peace.

He had grown to love the people of both villages and somewhere in his young and tender heart he knew that competition destroyed and that cooperation was less wasteful, allowing multiple agendas to co-exist, even flourish.

He dedicated his life to bringing the two villages together and after many years – sustained by faith and trust in human nature, but mostly naivety – he realised the unthinkable; members from the councils of both villages agreed to sit down in the same room and talk. Actually for the first few years they just ripped into each other about anything and everything, but having them face-to-face and unarmed was progress.

Rather than thinking like a mechanic, Adolf had to behave like a gardener. He was patient, and careful to make a note of everyone's demands and objections. Whenever proceedings got out of hand he calmly brought their attention back to the main point, the common ground, the dream they shared, the only thing they could agree on. Which was money. They all wanted to be rich...extremely rich...rich beyond imagination...much more than their neighbour.

Then the fighting started afresh.

Eventually Adolf judged it was time to unveil his master plan.

No-one was interested in peace, harmony and happiness, so he had to think of a different name for it, something that would fire the imaginations of the most bigoted of men. He called it *Megalo-Mountain.* It was the vision to build a lift network that linked the two ski areas to create a single Ski Paradise that would rival any in Europe.

"Over my dead body!" said one of the more articulate councillors, smacking his fist on the table. Prejudice was the fabric of his being, he couldn't just throw it away!

"A rising tide lifts *all* boats," said Adolf. There was a few moments of confused silence. It was an uncharacteristic slip and one he regretted. How could he be so foolish? Adolf had used a non-farming related metaphor.

The argument about who would have the biggest boat was ferocious.

Over my dead body turned out to more of a prophecy than a protestation because, after patiently facilitating seventeen years of negotiations in vain, it was only when the last of these die-hards died that the development could happen, that the villages could move out of the dark ages and become a single resort.

The tourists multiplied, property prices rocketed, businesses boomed and people of the neighbouring villages had conversations about the weather and even asked after each other's families.

But for some, even now, that "community spirit" is only *up on the hill* and based on financial reasoning. It is superficial, melting with the snow each spring.

"Helluva night," Ed said. The Bridge was still another 100 metres. The headlights of the snowplough blazed at his back and illuminated The Bridge and safety. Feeling the rush of adrenalin that was reserved for emergencies he was now running a small bit faster than was humanly possible. Behind him the engine roared as Schneider changed up a gear, the road trembled under his feet, his lungs cracked and splintered... But he made it. Just.

Having crossed The Bridge, Ed turned. The halogen eyes of the monster snow plough lit up the night as it noisily puffed diesel fumes. He shuffled on around the corner as far as the bus shelter, noticing his breath condensing to vapour as he said *That was brilliant.* He could smell pipe tobacco, he saw a ghost and passed out.

Ed recognised the stains on the ceiling. And the brown curtain.

"Thank fuck for that!" He was in his own bed.

"Trace... Trace!... get up we're gonna be late. Actually I'm pretty sure we're already late... Tracy?"

Daylight flooded the room. There was no coughing or abuse or panic for cigarettes. None of the usual morning sounds were sounding.

Ed rolled on to his side, levered himself up on his right elbow, opened his eyes again and waited for them to focus. But before that could happen he tumbled the short distance to the floor. He'd overcooked it this time.

He moved his hair out of his face. Tracy's bed was empty. Impossible to say if it had been slept in last night or not, it always looked the same. He could go over there and touch it, see if it was still warm, but just thinking about touching Tracy's bed made him feel nauseous.

He felt nauseous anyway.

He'd overcooked it this time.

Ed dropped his boxer shorts and slipped one leg out before sitting on the toilet. He always did that. If his feet were not wider than his shoulders when sitting on the pot he wasn't comfortable. The world fell out of his bottom. And the shower tray was full of wet, muddy clothes – which included his favourite boarding jacket and a pair of woollen socks with holes.

The plughole was blocked with slush and twigs and a pine cone. What…?

Images flashed through his mind; drinking test-tubes of phosphorescent liquid, standing on a chair singing *Sweet Child O Mine* better than Axle Rose and then a weather-beaten face with a halo of lightning-white curls and the glowing-red end of a pipe and…

He looked again at his sodden clothes in the shower tray, and at the slush and twigs and a pine cone blocking the plughole. Images flashed through his mind; he'd got caught out by the blizzard. Yes. And been chased by a snowplough? Now that bit must be fiction, much too Stephen King; his books were good, but in order to believe the story lines, to have it scare you, you have to suspend reality because that kind of shit doesn't really happen.

Sitting naked on the pot, he shivered. It was only a Wednesday. Or was it Thursday?

Ed and Tracy had first arrived in the resort three-and-a-half years ago. It was the first week in December, the resort was pre-season quiet, first snow had fallen, the sky was high and blue. The scene was pure and pristine just like Ed had dreamed. Blank canvas, full palette.

The lads went to meet their new boss. The news was bad; their room wasn't ready, it still needed to be cleaned. Ed and Tracy braced themselves, expecting to be given a mop, bucket and some rubber gloves but instead Boss Man apologised, explained how the cleaner had been delayed, said it would be ready in a few hours and asked if maybe they would like to go over to the bar on the other side of the ice rink?

"Say you are working with Johann, you will get locals' price."

Oh, okay.

The bar was a wooden building; it looked more like a stable.

Ed pushed open the heavy door. Inside it was dark and empty except for the barman. They sat on high stools around a wooden table in front of a small window. The glass was scratched and had little bubbles in it like old glass does. The mid-afternoon mid-winter sun shone through in a golden shaft of light.

It was all ahead of them. Cheers to this lads!

Ed was naked in the bathroom. He shivered. That first afternoon in the bar, when even the dust in the air had glittered and sparkled, seemed like a long time ago. He'd had some great moments over the years, but here he was sitting on the pot at the end of that rainbow.

It seemed the only happiness he ever found was sugar-coated suffering.

He was definitely late for work. The sun was higher than usual, it was warmer, the traffic was different. At the depot Tracy was sitting by the coffee machine, smiling like a Cheshire cat.

"Morning, Scrambles!" he said cheerfully.

Tracy. Cheerful? Strange.

"What's that tale the locals tell about the leprechaun blokey?" said Ed as he hit the Americano button.

"What? Aren't you going to ask me what happened last night?" replied Tracy, clearly disappointed.

"That is what I'm asking – do you know the story?"

"His name is Rolli. The only sightings are from people under severe duress like the Mountain Rescue Team when they were trapped in the Löwens Avalanche of '99. Some say he's one-metre-thirty tall but others argue he's more like one-sixty – apparently it depends on whether you include the heels of his cowboy boots and an impressive blonde afro. They say he lives in a cave on the north side and using Elven magic he can walk on soft snow without leaving prints. That's all I've got. Except he estivates from April to Halloween…"

Ed held his cup closer to his face and smelled the coffee.

"Aren't you going to ask me what *estivates* means?"

Ed was deep in thought, not even a chirpy Tracy could distract him.

"That's what I thought. And does Rolli smoke a pipe?" asked Ed.

"Every time."

"That's what I thought. It must be him then."

Ed told Tracy about running home, being nearly flattened by Schneider's snow plough and then being chased back across The Bridge before finally passing out in the bus shelter only to be saved by Rolli.

"I believe you," said Tracy

"Really?"

"Yep."

"But even I don't believe me."

"It all makes sense," said Tracy with that Cheshire cat smile and stroking his goatee, "…cos, you see, I reckon Schneider must have heard that his daughter was last seen leaving the bar with an Englander and then seeing you hurrying home at five in the morning he probably put one-and-one together and assumed it was you two. So while he nearly hammered you with his snow plough I was nailing his daughter to the headboard! I think I should get the audacity points this time!"

lunar boarding

Ed had been sober and eating three meals a day for nearly a week. As he walked back to work from the lunch restaurant he saw the cloud was lifting and the snowfall easing. The locals were saying that this time, when the weather clears, the conditions on the mountain would be the best in living memory.

That evening as Ed and Tracy left work an old black car was parked on the pavement outside the main door. It looked Russian. The engine was running. Two men got out, their hats pulled down low over their eyes. One of them opened a door and motioned for Ed and Tracy to slide into the back seat. The lads looked at each other and did as they were beckoned.

"You boys are in big troubles,"said the driver.

"No way!" said Ed

"Yes way. We're taking you to the glacier."

"Now?"

"Of course now. Tomorrow is too late. This night! Fresh snow, first tracks, y'know."

Ed felt a tingle that started at the back of his neck and ended in his heels. Lex the Nose and Man Who Smokes were snowboarding legends, wanted men; rumour had it they'd fled to the States...

"We are being on snow parole!"

"I can't, not tonight," said Tracy

"You what!" gasped Ed

"The DeFre Brothers have scored a forty-two inch flat screen TV in a top floor suite of Hotel Kenterhof. I'm bringing Formula 1, we're racing Monte Carlo for big money."

"Trace…it's Lex and Man Who Smokes…it aint gonna be small..." squeaked Ed.

"Sorry, lads, I've got plans."

Tracy got out of the car at Sylvie's Bar but somehow slipped on the snow and somehow Lex drove over his foot.

In his rear-view mirror Lex could see Tracy hopping and cursing and waving his fist. Man Who Smokes and Ed had turned in their seats and were laughing at Tracy as he hobbled after the car for a few steps before realising he was moving further away from where he wanted to be, giving up, and skulking back up the road to Sylvie's.

"Fuuck!" shouted Lex. He liked to swear in English; he said it felt more natural and gave it power. Ed and Man Who Smokes turned to face front again.

"Fuuck!" they shouted.

A bull was charging up the narrow street towards the car. Lex padded the brakes and while the car skidded to a stop on the snowy road he found reverse. The wheels spun before the tyres found traction and the car started moving backwards. Steam was billowing from the bull's nostrils, anger poured from its crossed and bloodshot eyes. It was on a leash. On the other end of the leash was Alfredo with a beetroot face and foaming with rage – his legs kicking wildly as he attempted to regain his feet.

The bull was charging at full speed but somehow Lex was driving backwards up the street a small bit faster. People jumped into snow drifts to escape the runaway reversing car that was being chased by a wild bull. They had already passed Tracy who appeared to be cheering the bull.

At the top of the village the road forked; Lex reversed at full speed up the uphill fork, while the bull pulled Alfredo down the downhill fork, his angry chants becoming fainter.

The car stood motionless, engine purring. The lads wowed and chuckled.

"I have eyes and now I am seeing!" said Lex, stroking the steering wheel. "Total geil!…Ich habe es noch nie geglaubt… Jesu!"

Ed could see a reflection of his shining face in the rear view mirror.

"This is Uncle Manny's car and is a DAF 66 which is having a belt-driven continuous variable transmission and is just saving our pig," said a stupefied Lex "We are escaping Alfredo's bull because of having a shifting variator."

Ed tapped Man Who Smokes on the shoulder and pointed at Lex.

"What he is saying is," said Man Who Smokes as he refilled his pipe, "if you are opening the front of this car you will be finding no gears only a rubber band with forwarts and backwarts. We are sitting in the only car ever built that can be coming backwarts the same speed as it can be doing forwarts!"

Ed was starting to appreciate what had just happened, the significance. The ramifications. Their only escape was reverse, and they just happened to be sitting in the fastest backwards driving production car in the world.

Cool.

The next morning Ed was walking to work. At the side of the road there was a huge pile of steaming shit next to a Mercedes S Class Coupe. The Mercedes belonged to one of the new boutique hotels. The shit was from Alfredo's cow shed. Alfredo was one of the few farmers who refused to sell out to developers.

As Ed approached, a fork-full of shit flew out of an opening in the ancient stone wall and landed on the pile. Ed waited for the next fork-full before deeming it safe enough to look in the window.

"Servus, Alfredo!" he said.

Alfredo looked up and grinned. He had two black eyes and a broken nose.

"Scrambled Egg!" he said leaning on his shit-fork and miming rapid sphincter movement with his right hand.

How did that happen? How is it that Alfredo is making fun of him – surely it should be the other way around...

The next fork full nearly caught Ed square in the face.

Their only escape had been reverse, and they just happened to be sitting in the fastest backwards driving production car in the world... Wow.

The bull had dragged Alfredo down the downhill fork in the road. The lads watched them disappear and did some high fives. Man Who Smokes lit the pipe, while Lex checked for oncoming traffic, switched to forward mode and drove back through the village. It was a Monday. On Mondays there was night skiing on the mountain above Landers. Higher again was The Glacier.

Ed, Lex and Man Who Smokes were on the chair-lift, being carried through the trees, higher into the darkness. As they got closer to the mid-station Ed could hear blasmusik and see the skiers in front of them getting off the lift, maybe to have a glühwein at the Landers Hütte before skiing down the floodlit piste back to the village.

At the lift station there was the silhouette of a man standing. As they approached Man Who Smokes croaked a greeting. The silhouette moved and made some sounds of reply; it was permission to stay on the lift, to travel onwards and upwards through the night to The Glacier.

They sailed into a bank of snow cloud. Ed opened his mouth and pristine bright white flakes dissolved on his tongue. There was no-one else around. Except for the trees. Then they were too high for trees. The clouds had cleared, the moon was full, the snow lay silent and perfect. It was a film set and they were the stars.

How ridiculous is man? Every day is sacred, the whole world is God's house.

They sat under the summit in silence. In awe. As he stepped into the board's bindings Ed tuned in to the luminescent world. Man Who Smokes tipped over the edge. Then Lex the Nose. Ed followed.

When time and space kiss, they make moments like this.

They returned to the land of clocks, to the artificial light and superficial joys of the Landers Hütte.

season's end

He opened an eye. It was already light outside. The lace curtain moved, the window had been ajar all night, yet it was not cold. The end of a season was always tough for Ed. He worked with his head down, checking pay slips and weighing options for the summer.

During the lunch break he sat on a bench in the middle of a growing island of green grass. Another winter had happened. Was over.

Change is continuous but there must be a tipping point. Imagine being so finely tuned to nature that you could smell the exact moment when spring begins, or summer ends…or a life becomes a death…

It was comforting to Ed that he could witness this in person. Not by looking at a calendar or hearing about it from someone else – but opening his eyes and having it look at him. This way he could grieve. Which was ironic. He'd been willing the winter away and now he was experiencing loss.

Loss? Maybe because he was coming to the end of something and was no wiser than when he started. He'd been watching other people on vacation for months; holidays were not the answer, neither was living a life we want to escape from.

The next day Tracy suggested they have lunch at the panorama restaurant on the top of the mountain and watch some people sliding on slush.

They were dressed in t-shirts, not just to show off their tattoos, but because it was warm. Hot even. The boys silently filled their trays with carbohydrates and beer, and took a seat by the window. Sitting in the panorama.

He was a very tall man, his black coat reached his knees. He wore thick-lensed bi-focal glasses.

"Can I thit with you?" he said in perfect English (apart from the impediment).

The boys say nothing. They have said nothing since they arrived. How does he even know they speak English? Bi-focal Man sat down next to Ed, almost on Ed. Ed slid over to regain some space.

Bi-focal Man's curly hair was brushed flattish and there was a large pair of binoculars hanging around his neck. Ed looked over his shoulder, wondering who is pulling the strings, or where the hidden camera was.

Bi-focal Man put his red purse on the table next to Tracy's tray of food and took one of Tracy's chips. He dipped Tracy's chip in Tracy's mayonnaise and put it up to his mouth which was already chewing in anticipation.

Ed moved his beer to the far end of the table.

Tracy lost his appetite. He sat back and reached for his cigarettes. The man watched Tracy take out a cigarette, spin it in his fingers, put it in his mouth, reach for his zippo and spark a flame before saying;

"Thigarette thmoking is not allowed."

"Thorry," said Tracy with the cigarette between his lips "Perhaps I thould wait until you thinished my thood."

Bi-Focal Man pointed to a *No Smoking* sign above Tracy's head.

The lighter blazed in Tracy's right hand as he looked up at the sign. He leaned back in the chair so it was balanced on its two hind legs, so his head was a few inches inside the smoking zone, and put the flame to the cigarette which he held like Winston Churchill holding a cigar.

Bi-focal Man studied Tracy, his mouth open wide and full of food.

"What?…" said Tracy from inside a cloud of smoke. "Carry on. I don't mind if you eat while I thmoke."

When these kind of things happen the veil of reality appears very thin, the back-drop of reason falls away, these people are peep-holes into parallel universes, messengers from the other side… or maybe just a season's worth of hangovers and highs have all come home to roost at the same time? Ed looked around again, waiting for someone to jump out and say it was all a prank. But no-one jumped out.

The world kept turning just the same.

It was definitely time for Ed to get off.

return

eight o'clock

The evening guests for the wedding were arriving at eight o'clock. Ed needed it to be eight o'clock and he needed Tracy to be on time. They'd have a Jagermeister or two and after a few beers get the DJ to play something good – maybe The Smiths, *Big Mouth Strikes Again.* They could pull up some flowers from the hotel garden, stuff them down the back of their trousers and have a dance.

Even before eight o'clock some of the evening guests started to arrive including some old friends, people he could talk to and understand. Except they were on good behaviour, or impressing their new partner, or talking about careers or mortgages or the price of nappies.

Ed was keeping half an eye on the door; some families entered, a girl couple, a group of lads…then a man came in wearing black rim glasses. Ed smiled, it reminded him of Tracy's nerd impression. This man stood tall, was wearing a sharp suit and pushing a buggy, arm in arm with a very attractive woman. He was happy. Ed could tell that from a distance. The woman said something that made her man smirk. Which is when Ed recognised him. That *is* Tracy!

Ed hesitated. But Tracy saw him, came over and gave him a big hug. Tracy had never given Ed a hug before. He was introduced to Becky, they'd been married nine months. The baby was a little older than that.

"Is that a zoot suit?" Becky said to Ed.

"Yep," said Tracy helpfully "He had it tailor-made in Nepal. Isn't it, Scrambles?"

"It is. I did," said Ed.

They sat at a table and Ed told them bits about the day. Other people who recognised one or both of them called over and everyone was introduced again.

Becky had done all the driving and the baby needed feeding; she would take her up to the room.

"Spence, I'm gonna head up with Baby now, me love," Becky said.

"Okay Becks," Tracy said before kissing his daughter on the crown of her head and rubbing noses with Becky. He watched his beautiful wife disappear through the door as if she was someone else's beautiful wife.

"Spencer?"

"Yeah."

"No, I mean, *Spencer*? Since when are you Spencer again?"

"Oh, well, Becks wanted to call our daughter Tracy and so we just thought it would be simpler all round."

"But Spencer is a war criminal."

"No. Actually he isn't. Wasn't. Cos, you see, Becks reckons we all make mistakes and the most important thing is I never set out to harm anybody. It was not malicious, not even conscious – just naivety to an almost unimaginable but ultimately forgiveable degree – so it becomes a crime of ignorance and there I'm not alone. The important thing is that I acknowledge my wrongs and resolve never to repeat them..."

He'd said that last bit like he was reading a script.

"So that's the theory, but she also she did some hard research and, you see, I was in L Division, making parts for the Triniton X970 and that warhead was never deployed, as in dropped, as in exploded, as in killing anyone, and now they have all been decommissioned which means they never will! So you see, in fact there are no armies of innocent victims in the afterlife waiting for me with their vengeance sharpened. There is no karmic bomb about to fall on my head, well not in relation to my professional activity anyway. Isn't that great!" Tracy, or rather Spencer, smiled into space. "So I don't have to hate myself any more. I can be happy..."

It sounded to Ed that Tracy had maybe done some pyramid flipping of his own.

"Mostly happy anyway," he continued, "It's difficult to trust what is happening now without dragging up my shit from the past and flinging it at the future. I can still sabotage my well-being in the most imaginative ways. Sometimes it seems a part of me is just more comfortable with problems. Meeting Becks has been like being, well y'know, my second chance, I nearly said *born again* but that would give you the wrong impression."

Without asking for it, Ed got their story.

"I was doing some painting for a friend-of-a-friend. He had me standing in front of a beautiful teak wall, he put a tin of oil-based paint in my hand and told me to cover it. I stood there looking at it for a while, dipped the hairs of the brush into the paint and held it out towards the wood. I really didn't want to do it, so I didn't. I dropped the brush into the can, watched it sink, and walked."

Tracy had walked down the street lost in thought. He was feeling that little bit of a tremble you get when you are angry and suddenly unemployed and owe rent. Dark clouds swarmed. The first few drops of rain fell. Then it came down in buckets. He ducked into a doorway for shelter, then peered through the window; it was a bookshop, with a few comfortable looking chairs, hardwood shelves and ornate lamps. It looked like the cabin of an old ship. Maybe they had comics. He went inside.

His glasses steamed up so he took them off to wipe them on his sagging woollen jumper. Someone asked him if he was looking for something in particular. When he put his glasses back on he was looking at Becky.

"I was blind and then I could see. Never seen anything like her before though. The shelves were stacked with sentences but I couldn't find one.

"I just made some noises and nodded a few times. Funny, I have seen you like that loads of times, never thought it could happen to me! Anyway she suggested I might like to put some price labels on a stack of books.

"She took me by the elbow and sat me down. I'd only done about ten books when a guy came in wearing a fluorescent vest. He was from a local support group that finds work placements for people living with intellectual disabilities. His name was Dave. I was doing his job!

"Well this sort of snapped me out of it. I apologised and got out of his chair, and apologised to Becky who thought it was all good for a laugh and I left, didn't I? It was still lashing rain."

Tracy was not sure his apology was clear and sincere enough, so the next morning he went back. With a bar of chocolate for Dave and bunch of flowers for Becky.

When he got there Becky was busy so he pretended to be book shopping. There were books about everything. And about nothing. In the back there was a conservatory extension with a solid fuel stove where they served salads, cake and coffee. He had a refill of coffee and second slice of cake, shuffling his chair around so he could eye Becky without it looking too obvious. Then she came over and sat at his table. "What kind of books do you read?" she asked him.

"Me? Read?"

"Yes. You read?"

"Mostly magazines. And CD inserts."

She smiled. Wow! He must do that again. Jokes. He needed to be funny.

"Okaaay. What kind of work do you do?" she asked.

"I'm a painter. Well, I used to be a painter. Not an artist, y'know walls..." Then he explained about the day before, how he'd not really been himself because he'd just made himself redundant.

Becky served some customers but came back to his table. She was holding a book. "You should read this." Tracy flicked to the back of the book: 219 pages to get into this girl's pants? It was worth it.

He was in a comfortable chair, started reading then and there, and next thing he knew the shop was shutting. That night he fell asleep thinking about finishing the book.

When he'd finished the book – soon after lunch the following day – he rushed back to the bookshop. He had to give a report. The shop was busy. His coffee went cold. He didn't dare smoke. Which made him nervous. He was already nervous.

"So, tell me..." she said.

He had some lines rehearsed but they reversed out of his mouth. Another customer needed serving, which bought him some time. When she next sat down he rattled off enough coherent information to prove he'd read the book.

"Did you enjoy it?"

Enjoy? A book? Again she had to serve a customer. When she came back he'd ask her out for sure.

When she came back she was holding another book.

"Try this one."

This book was fat and heavy and the cover looked boring. She was amused by his faked enthusiasm. That smile again...

He decided rather than read the book he'd look at some reviews and memorise a few of the salient points. Two days later he went back to the bookshop. It was her day off but she'd left a note. For him! Probably a telephone number. He managed to get outside the door before he opened it.

"*Lies this early in our friendship are not a good sign. See you Monday.*"

Monday was after the weekend. Three days away. He'd have to read the book.

Reviewing The Third Book with Becky he tried to talk like he was someone else, because *he* was not good enough.

The Fourth Book was his last. She, this, it, was doing his head in.

For The Fifth Book she wanted to know how reading it had made him *feel*. How it made him feel *and* why. Giving up smoking was nothing compared to this. He had mostly given up smoking.

About six weeks after they first met, and between The Seventh and Eighth Book, he had to work in the bookshop with Becky's mother while Becky went on a hen weekend.

She showed Tracy how to work the till one more time. Then she went out the door wearing black thigh-high boots and holding a fluffy pink handbag.

Tracy paused in his telling of the story to look apologetically at Ed. "And, yeah, sorry about not inviting you to the wedding. Or even letting you know it was happening. We didn't have any guests except Beck's mum and she invited herself.

"There was this thing with our wedding rings, I have to tell you this. We got married in a hurry, it was just busy, lots of stuff going on. I have stayed in touch with Zeb from my body art days, he makes jewellery, we decided to get him to make matching wedding bands with blessing mantras engraved on them. So Zeb sent me sizing strips to measure our fingers – you choose the hole that fits your ring finger, that's your size – we did it carefully even though it was easy because there wasn't time or the money to replace them if they were wrong. We sent that off, ordered those. I didn't have a suit of course and Becks didn't have a dress. Anyway the rings arrived, just in time, so we tried them on. And they were only too big! Couldn't believe it. Baggy rings! We decided to keep them just for the ceremony, so we'd have something to give each other, and worry about it after. Anyway, on the day, when we came to exchange rings they fitted! Both of them. And they still fit. Is that cool or what?

"Now I work in the bookshop. I make the quiche and mix the salads and sometimes recommend books to people. That's another thing; when we went to book the wedding date, the registrar lady was filling in forms, and when she asked my occupation I just said *Poet.* And she wrote it down! Just like that. Me, a poet! Ha!"

seeing

Tracy was at the bar, Ed was observing the crowd. Henrietta, the girl from dinner with the kookaburra laugh, was walking across the dance floor. Talk of the devil-like thoughts. She wore a white dress, it fitted her better than well. Ed studied it carefully from neck to knee; under the dance-floor lights he could see it had three layers. The outer layer was longer and like a veil, the inner layer was a knee-length skirt, maybe Egyptian cotton, through which he could see the secret layer, a mini, probably silk.

As she crossed the floor two lads went to block her path and made it look like an accident. Ed had seen these two arriving by helicopter, one he recognised, he'd seen him somewhere before, on TV maybe. Henrietta turned sideways and glided by them like they didn't exist. That's it! The one he recognised, he remembered now, he plays rugby for England. The two lads watched as she walked on, and then looked at each other, and then at her back, before continuing on their journey to the bar.

There's something unusual about that one, thought Ed. She had more class than this exclusive establishment and all the other guests put together, yet she talks with her mouth full and laughs like a jungle parrot.

Tracy flicked beer in Ed's face. Then followed his stare. "What kind of woman wears a white dress to a wedding – I mean, unless she's the bride?"

"She can't be the bride, she's wearing fourteen hole Doc Martin boots with red roses embroidered on them," replied Ed.

"Fair point, Scrambles. I'm married now but back in the day I wouldn't still be sitting here listening to you I'd be over there getting my tatts out. You should mosey over, it'd be a real treat to see you in action again, I've forgotten what a decent blow-out looks like."

"You can't bait me with that sort of talk, Trace. These days I keep life simple, which means staying away from emotional rollcr-coasters."

"Ed-ward. Where's your audacity?"

"You mean an extra-ordinary luck combined with overbearing pride and self-importance, a lack of prudence, propriety and convention? Good question – gone forever I hope. Audacious maybe good to watch but it's no fun to be. That's what sent me to the cliff top. No, I'm working on something much more authentic and resilient than an audacity shield – chasing a girl like that would jeopardise everything."

He'd been waiting for an opportunity; now seemed good. Ed told Tracy about the day's insight – the image of the pyramid – and how from a more settled place he could see all the restlessness and insecurity, how he had lived his life guided by a voice he never knew existed.

"Some things don't change," puffed Tracy.

"No, Trace, this is not disappearing-up-my-own-crack rhetoric. This is practical and relevant."

"Thus spoke Zarathustra!"

"Sara who?" Ed was wrong footed.

"Zarathustra. It's Friedrich Nietzsche. *If I wanted to shake this tree with my hands I should be unable to do it. But the wind which we cannot see, torments it and bends it where it wishes. It is invisible hands that torment and bend us the worst.*"

Ed looked at the person in front of him quoting Nietzsche.

Where the hell was Tracy?

gazebo two

However posh a wedding celebration begins it usually ends the same. And the end is nigh when the DJ plays *Thunderstruck*. It had been great to see Tracy but not in the way Ed had expected. Tracy had gone up to his room soon after the music finished; he had to be up early, they were leaving straight after breakfast to meet some of Beck's relatives at an antiques fair.

Ed was back in the gazebo reviewing the day – he had just lost his way temporarily that's all, it was an invitation to grow. He reassured himself with a favourite Thomas Merton quote: *Souls are like athletes, that need opponents worthy of them, if they are to be tried and extended and pushed to the full use of their powers, and rewarded according to their capacity.* Coming to the wedding was not a mistake, it had given him all the resolve he needed to go back to his cliff top and finish the journey – to let the pyramid fall onto its base. And stay there. There was no room for any more resolve, he was overflowing with it.

All his life he had lived in his head and been balancing on an edge. It was the devil he knew, and he knew no alternative. But his recent experience and the image of the pyramid had given him confidence that there was nowhere to fall. Who would have thought, who *could* have thought, that the freedom he'd always dreamt of was, and had always been, inside of himself? Waiting. Ready.

It was up to him now; his whole past and the sum of all his

aspirations for the future can be bound together to make a fictional on-point personality.

Or scattered on the out breath.

He exhaled. A good one. After all the frenetic activity and toothy laughter of the party it was such a relief to be sitting quietly by himself. He *had* changed. *This* is how he enjoyed himself these days. Under a full moon on the last Saturday in August he felt very awake.

Some people like being in a queue, it's comforting, somehow proving that they are in the right place at the right time, and engaged in valid activity. For Ed it was almost always the opposite. Like now. It was the middle of the night, the whole world was in bed and asleep, but not him.

He kept coming back to the silence. It was so big. And surprising. Even when a donkey brayed somewhere in the same valley – loud, long and loaded with loneliness – it did not change the silence, it enhanced it. Like jewels around a beautiful neck. Ed smiled. You can be at the poshest hotel in the country, on the planet even, but a farmer can still put a lonely donkey in the field next door.

In the same way he can't control what arises in his mind – or appears in the world around him – but he can give it space.

Someone was coming. Ah, he didn't feel like being moved on, or sharing his space. His exit was blocked. Oh who cares. *Let it in.*

It was Henrietta, the girl from dinner with the three-layer dress and the kookaburra laugh. She was carrying a wine bottle. When Henrietta saw Ed she hesitated, then continued her approach.

"You're the one who was dancing with flowers down the back of your trousers," she said.

"And you met your second husband trying to get out of your first wedding dress."

"Ah, actually no. I'm the one who told that story but that's all it is. At dinner I was surrounded by people who thought they were sitting at a high table in life because of who they are or something they have done. I've seen too many kind and talented people struggle to make ends meet to believe it's that simple. I was just sticking a pin in their pretence. So no, I'm not married and never have been, the fifty-two buttons thing is something I overheard at the last wedding I went to."

"A convincing act."

"Well thank you. My parents would be pleased to know drama school was not a complete waste of money. I'm Henri," she said, holding out a hand.

"Is that for real or a stage name?"

"For real," she said, laughing (like a mountain stream).

"Ed," he said taking her right hand but looking at the wine bottle in her left.

"It's empty," she said. "I wanted to walk in the gardens, brought this for self-protection, in case my jungle-bird laugh wasn't enough." She tossed the bottle, it landed silently in the rose garden.

"But now you are unarmed," Ed said.

"True, but you're wearing an azure blue suit and drinking from a silver tea set. I figure I can look after myself. Were you an invited guest at the wedding?"

"Sure, why else would I be here?"

"I thought maybe you were to entertain the kids – a balloon artist or something."

Ed opened his mouth but the words of his reply were not ready.

"It's okay, I like people who wear their uniqueness on their sleeve," she continued. "So-called normal people unnerve me, their strangeness is concealed, waiting, ready to surprise you."

That sounded dangerously like Henri could be interested

in a balloon-artist boyfriend. Ed quickly reminded himself he was famous for misjudging situations of this nature; she was out of his league anyway, he wouldn't even try, he'd just be himself. That's what The Pyramid was all about. Not trying to be some-one or something else. Comfortable with who you are. As you are.

Henri was still standing. She gestured toward the tea tray on the bench next to Ed.

"Oh right. Yeah." He lifted it up so she could sit down.

"Is there any left?" she asked picking up the tea pot, swirling it to feel for quantity and placing her left hand against it to test the temperature. She had a lapis lazuli ring on her middle finger.

"May I?" she asked.

"Yeah, I guess. Except I only have the one..."

Henri lifted the pot and tipped the tea into the side of her mouth like she was smoking a pipe. Difficult to do that, drink tea direct from the pot, with grace, and oozing hotness.

She crossed her legs, leaned back and exhaled. "Bit stewy but refreshing all the same. It's a treat to be among the trees isn't it. It's been a funny day, don't know what I was expecting really."

"I had a lot of expectations too," said Ed, "me and Tracy were tight and getting back together after all this time. I was looking forward to it. But Tracy has changed. He's now called Spencer. And he got married to a pretty woman – and all without telling me."

"Wow. And you never suspected anything? I can see how that would be a shock. How long ago did you split up with her?"

"Split up with who?"

"Tracy."

"No, Tracy, is a *he*."

"Yes, I understand, now Tracy is a man called Spencer, but before that, when he was your girlfriend, and called Tracy..."

Ed brought Henri up to speed with the Ed-Tracy story during which a night porter on his rounds picked up the tea tray and brought them a jug of pink lemonade that was left over from the day. Just like that. And no charge. Life gets cheaper the richer you become.

"So what's next?" she asked.

"I'm between things, house-sitting on a cliff-top in Ireland." Ed told her how he'd reached the end of the road with travelling, and with just about everything.

"It sounds like you'd ticked all the boxes on your bucket list but weren't dead yet. Or happy."

"Something like that."

"I'm just back from the Alps," she offered. "A place my brother and I had visited the year before he died. I always needed to go back but it took until now to actually do it. We had camped in an apple orchard and swum in the lake, ate Italian ice-cream and relaxed in the sun. The trip was my birthday present, I was eighteen. It was a happy time in what was going to be a happy life. So I went back there to remember him, and to remember happiness.

"I know trying to re-visit something special is always a risk, well, they had cut down almost all of the orchard and paved it with concrete, there was nearly nowhere to sink a peg and hardly any shade. The sun beat down and the heat came up at you in a bright glare. There were no apples to eat for breakfast or lunch, or with wine and cheese in the evening, the magic was gone, the faeries had moved on. There were only retired people in motor-homes playing cards or looking into the shimmering space.

"I was ready to turn around and drive on but remembered that's how it had been the first time; my brother and I had arrived in the rain and I had wanted to leave already but Darren, that's my brother, said *Wait up there Henri girl, what's the hurry, there is nowhere to run to, give it a chance*, and the next day the sun came out and we had an amazing week.

"So this time I gave myself some more time, I'd been on the road for days and was tired, so I pitched my tent under the last remaining tree and sat with the grey-haired folk while they told me about a favourite dog and the camper vans they'd owned and the places they'd been. I had stone-baked pizza after long swims and smiled with love for my brother and cried because he died.

"Dig it Henri! he used to say to me. *Moments are like tomatoes on a vine; fresh and vibrant, bursting with flavour. We like our food fresh, that way it's nutritious. Why then do we put up with processed experience? We turn our everyday into a lifeless ready-meal – wrapped up in our preferences and prejudices.* He called it *Locked Out Syndrome.* He said that's a big reason why people enjoy their holidays, and why he travelled a lot, because when we are somewhere new we bring a different quality of attention to ordinary things – like what we are eating or who we are talking to. When we walk down a foreign street our senses are open and alive.

"*Dig it Henri!* And with him I did, he helped me see magic in the everyday. I've lost that since he's gone. Now the only time I feel alive is when I'm nearly not. While I was out there this time I did an Accelerated Free Fall course, that's what they call skydiving now. I'm going to get into wingsuit flying."

"Seriously?" said Ed, "I read an article on that recently – the fatality stats are mad."

"Sure, there's an assumed risk and accidents happen."

"No, pony trekking is assumed risk, wingsuit flying is more like a death wish."

"Whatever. You can wrap me up in cotton wool when I'm in my coffin, not while I'm still breathing. I would rather give my life to something I love than have it taken from me." She finished abruptly. And wasn't breathing. Then she did breathe.

"Phew! I had to watch those sparkling eyes fade to nothing. I loved him very much."

She wiped away a tear and sniffed, then smiled at Ed as if to say *I'm over it.*

After some respectful silence Ed searched himself for the courage to ask the question. They'd only just met. It could completely backfire. He decided he didn't mind. He'd take the chance. Here goes....

"Why does everybody have to be strange?" he said.

"What?"

"Well earlier you said that normal people are still strange, they are just better at hiding it."

"Did I? I suppose that does sound like me. Well because there's no such thing as normal. How can there be? Human existence inspires dis-ease and we either express it or suppress it. Like the people sitting at dinner this evening, hiding behind their champagne and cologne. Take away their make-up and manicures and who are they really? We all do it, colour our self with qualities, touching our self up moment to moment, another day another coat, keeping it vivid. We look in the mirror and we see something. *This is who I am.* People talk to us and we talk back. But there's nothing there really, just layers of stories. At the first sign of trouble it all gets blown away."

This sounded suspiciously similar to Ed's new Pyramid-on-Point Theory. He told Henri about balancing the pyramid – a very essential version,

"Yes, possibly, something like that," she said. "I would see myself more as a Christmas tree. Balancing on the angel end. And in a high wind."

" Okay, so why would we persist in that? No, specifically, why do *you* persist in that?"

"Well, that's because occasionally life presents me with perfect moments, you know *peak experiences* – in pyramid-speak you'd probably call it freak equilibrium – which are unforgettably good. Personally I put up with all kinds of shite in an attempt to get there again, in fact I pro-actively live on an edge just to repeat the feeling, and will continue to for the rest of my little life. What else is there?" She didn't wait for an answer. "When are you leaving?" she asked.

"I'm hitching so whenever I can get a ride, I guess."

"Where are you going?"

"Swansea. I'm taking the ferry back to Ireland."

"I'll take you, I can call in on my folks, we'll get some breakfast on the way."

"Sounds like a plan! I just need to leave a note for Tracy."

"Meet you in the car park then."

ride

Ed was going to leave a note but as he approached reception Tracy was coming down the stairs holding a crying baby.

"Trace, I've got a lift so I'm heading off already, great to see you, and meet the family. A bit of a shock but hey…"

Ed wanted to give Tracy a hug or at least shake his hand but there was a noisy baby in the way and Tracy didn't look like he was in the mood. He was grey with tiredness, quite different from the night before.

"We'll have the house mostly finished by the spring," said Tracy over the crying as they walked across the entrance foyer to the front door. "There'll be a spare room, you should come over and visit."

"Yeah, yeah, maybe," said Ed, "Although spring will be busy in the poly-tunnel. Maybe you all could come over to Ireland – get yourselves some fresh air and scenery!"

But Tracy wasn't listening, he was looking over Ed's shoulder and into the car park. The baby had gone quiet too.

Ed turned in time to see Henri hitch up her dress; he got a glimpse of the early-risen sun lighting up the perfect half-moon of her bronzed buttock as she slid into black leather. Next to her was a white Ducati motorcycle.

"Scrambles."

"Yuh."

"Is that your lift?"

"Yuh."

"Where's your bag?" Henri asked.

Ed opened his jacket to reveal a toothbrush in the breast pocket.

"It's not polite you know…"

"What?"

"Staring at a girl you hardly know getting changed in a public car park."

"Oh. Okay. Sorry."

He faked turning away while she removed the dress over her head and put on her jacket.

"Do you ride?" she asked

"What?"

"Bikes? Do you? Have you ever…?"

"Oh. Yes I do. Er, no not really, my experience is more mopeds."

She hadn't zipped up her jacket fully yet. "Just relax. And follow me. Got it?"

"Roger that."

Henri zipped herself away and passed Ed a helmet. He put it gently down on the ground, removed his suit jacket, did up the buttons and put it on over his head, back-to-front.

"It'll stop the insects going down my front," he said.

Henri had her helmet on, she tilted her head to the side, her expression hidden behind the visor.

Birdsong was replaced by a 900cc Italian rooster.

As Henri accelerated out of the car park, the back wheel sprayed gravel into the water fountain.

moped diaries

Wales was experiencing a heat-wave. It was twenty-two degrees and the roads were melting. Ed was eighteen and his hormones were in the red. He'd seen Rosanna every day of the summer and made her a promise; as soon as he passed his motorbike test they would ride off into the setting sun.

There were three of them on the motorcycle training course; Geoff, Matt and Ed. They sat astride their bikes on the windy, disused airfield facing Alex the Instructor.

They dabbed their feet on the ground, knocked cones, collided with tyres and went on the grass until Alex couldn't take any more. This was not some kind of game – riding bikes is the stuff of life! He ordered them to turn off their engines. It was time for a pep talk.

"Listen up, boys. If it's not right it's wrong. Right?"

"Right."

"Right."

"Right."

"You 'ave to observate more. And become more fam... famil...get to know your bike."

"Right."

"Right."

"Right."

After another hour of cones and tyres he seemed happy to

take the training trio down the coast road. Alex was in a tailor-made black leather suit, his 1100cc Triumph throbbing away quietly under him. The boys all wore nylon rain-trousers flapping in the wind as they screwed their worn-out 125cc machines for all they were worth but were still in no danger of exceeding any speed limit – even going through the villages.

Alex pulled over at Morgan's Café before they went into town. Morgan's had recently featured in *Biker*, the most honourable of all the monthly bike mags. The lads followed Alex inside. He flicked his left hand at them indicating they were to sit on a table in the alcove, while he went to join his mates at the big table in the window. Their teas and bacon sandwiches arrived almost immediately.

Geoff had eaten his sandwich. He sat with his elbows on the table and his chin in his hands. And sighed. He needed his bike test so he could get to work cheaply, so there was enough money at the end of the week to support his wife and two young kids.

That's kind of tough. No open road and mountain passes and riding off into the sunset for him then.

Back out in the car park Alex seemed much more relaxed and happy. He'd been talking about bikes with people who understood bikes, and he was full of tea and bacon sandwich.

"Nought to 'undred *and* back to a stop in 6.3 seconds," he told them, looking at his machine and rubbing his crotch.

They headed into town in a little procession. Alex glided like a spirit being while they revved and meandered and fiddled and fumbled their way through the traffic. They lost Geoff.

"Fuck 'im," said Alex at the next stop. "I used to chase 'em but it's a waste of fuel and time. It's 'is own stupid fault, 'e'll find us. Or not."

Ed did an over enthusiastic hill-start as he approached the roundabout on the brow of the hill. He nearly collided with a motorcycle entering the roundabout from his right. It was Geoff.

Ed looped around and came back to Alex who was hopping around on the pavement, banging his fist against his helmet. His good mood was over.

"Go over there and park up next to my bike," he screamed at Ed.

It was difficult to hear with all the engine noise and wearing a helmet .

"What did you say?" Ed shouted back. "Did you say I could have a go on your bike?"

"Fuck off!" said an apoplectic Alex.

Alex took some tablets and five minutes later the boys were ducklings-in-a-line following him down the road. They pulled over at the emergency stop practice spot. Waiting there, sitting on the kerb next to a little motorbike, was a woman dressed in leathers. Neither she nor her clothing looked new. She took a last draw on her cigarette and flicked it in the direction of a drain.

Alex lifted his visor. "Look, I don't want you 'ere today," he said to the woman.

"Tough. I called the office and they said it was okay."

"They didn't. Go away!"

"They did. No!"

Alex had mentioned that some people took failing their bike test really hard. It was expensive and required more training and form-filling and of course there was the dented ego. Who knows why they failed; it could be extreme weather, heavy traffic, a technical fault on the bike or the examiner could be having a bad day…or it could be they endangered the lives of other road-users.

Whatever the problem had been on Test Day it was usually the instructor who would receive all the flak, and the failed candidates were familiar with the training runs and test routes so would often show up to vent some frustration and apportion blame. Leather Woman must be one of them.

Alex tried to ignore Leather Woman and continued with a description of the emergency stop procedure. He paused to consider which word would be best to use next, which is when Leather Woman jumped in with how she had been cheated on her big day by screwing up her emergency stop.

"The front fuckin brake failed, so I stood on the back fuckin brake didn't I, fuckin bike skidded and they fuckin failed me!"

"Shut up you. Now, where was I?"

"Don't *shut up you* me..."

Ed was mystified, clearly this was not the first time these two had crossed swords. Why was Alex putting up with any of this? Leather woman was trouble – pure and simple. Eventually Alex sent her once round the block, said he'd speak to her when she got back. Leather woman put on her helmet, kicked her little bike into life and buzzed off up the road.

"They needed a bog roll to list all the things that woman done wrong on 'er test," puffed Alex as Leather Woman disappeared around the corner. "Right lads, don't 'ang about, follow me." Alex set off in the opposite direction.

At the U-turn training point they stopped again. Alex tried to disorientate his students by throwing in a surprise Highway Code question. He looked at Ed;

"You're riding down the motorway and something falls off your bike. What do you do?"

Alex's trick worked. Ed was wrong footed. The test wasn't until tomorrow; he was planning to look at the highway code that evening.

Luckily Geoff dived in for some brownie points. "You stop at the nearest emergency telephone box and call the police."

"Yes," said Alex clearly relieved. "Last week an Irish fella said 'e would go back and pick it up, 'e didn't like the idea of getting the police involved."

A high pitched noise came round the corner. It was Leather Woman in the wrong gear.

"Ah for fuck's sake…"

This time she parked in the road. Removed her helmet and they went at it, f-ing and blinding as loud as human lungs can go. Alex had his oily finger an inch from the end of her nose. "You're a fuckin menace. I'm 'aving nothing more to do with you."

"You will y'know, cos tomorrow I will pay 'em and request you."

"Bugger off!"

"Bugger off yourself! And don't come 'ome tonight expecting food – you can cook your own fuckin supper!"

The next day Ed failed his bike test. It was a list as long as a bog-roll. On his way home he stopped off again at Dai's Bikes on the edge of the industrial estate.

He stood in front of a bike at the back of the shop; the seat was ripped, the frame re-painted with blue hammerite, except for the green bits. And the petrol tank was rose red. Hence the name. "Goodbye, Rosanna," he said.

Ed had been a teenager then. And it would have been nearly ten years later when he next got his leg over a moped.

◆

Ed was finishing a summer of river-guiding in Austria and had decided it was his last. There had been *an incident.*

Rivers are graded according to difficulty. Flat, slow moving water is Grade 1 while Grade 6 is extreme conditions/danger to life. The rivers they rafted were usually Grade 3. Waves, thrills, excitement, splashing – but nothing too serious.

But river running is very similar to life in general – it's all about speed and angle. If you get it right it looks easy, but if your approach is wrong something simple can get very complicated. Which is why some river guides, rather than give a white-water section one grade to reflect its difficulty, would give two values; the first for navigating the correct line, and a second for the seriousness of the consequences if you screwed up. So the line could be Grade 3, but if you screwed it up the consequences could be Grade 5.

The two-value system added a little colour and reality to the situation, made some allowance for variables such as the level of the river, the mood and competence of the crew, and the quality of the guide's hangover.

However, we live in a world where you can break your neck stepping off a pavement and drown in a puddle of water so it's all bullshit really.

The Incident was close to the end of the season. Ed was guiding a raft down a Grade 4 section of river with Grade 5+ consequences if you missed the line. That day Ed was miles from getting it right and hit The Tombstone. One of his crew fell out and was washed under the raft. She didn't re-surface.

The whole river rushed at The Tombstone, the water flowing up and around the rock, but also under it. If she had been flushed under the rock she may not be found until the river levels dropped to their mid-winter low. He barked orders at the seven remaining crew. The raft bounced around The Tombstone and they paddled into the safety of an eddy. She was still under the water. Ed watched and waited, he needed to see a red helmet come to the surface now...

He fixed a reassuring face to greet the concerned looks of his crew.

Let me off this one and I'll stop tempting fate he prayed.

Then she surfaced, her open mouth was as big as her whole head, Ed span the raft and rejoined the current as she floated towards them. Her friends shouted excitedly while Ed hauled her aboard, answering her horrified look with feigned confidence. She had been underwater for less than ten seconds which had been the equivalent of several lifetimes.

Around this time two of Ed's raft-guide colleagues had been invited to join an expedition to run a river in Afghanistan (there was a brief lull in the war that was ravaging the country). Little was known about the river, and it would be a first descent by kayak, but from aerial footage they had been able to discern that at one point the river disappeared – it flowed into a hole in the ground and re-emerged at the bottom of a cliff several miles downstream – so they would have to pull off the river and portage the subterranean section before resuming. You wouldn't want to get that wrong.

Ed had a nightmare about being flushed into the bowels of the earth...Sensation seeking never ends. The next thrill could be the one to kill him.

How much luck can one life hold?

He would quit while he was alive and before he killed anyone else. He was a retired raft guide. Decision made. Until he received a fax from Ricky and Steve-O who were setting up a high-ropes course in a forest in the Dominican Republic. They had met a bloke who was looking to hire river guides.

Adventure sports was an expanding industry and getting into

a country early was always more fun. Rafting in the Caribbean? He didn't even know there was such a thing. You can't end your career without having been a river guide in the Caribbean, can you?

He had made a promise. But the promise was a last *Austrian* season. He replied to the fax.

Even while he was in the air, as he watched the little aeroplane motif slowly stutter across a map of the Atlantic Ocean on the screen at the front of the cabin, inching closer to the American-end of the Atlantic, there was no excitement, he was just ticking a box. His head hadn't changed, so he would make rafting in the Caribbean the same as rafting anywhere else.

One day just two months later, he finished his last Caribbean river trip and had planned to spend the last week of his stay on the coast; not luxuriating with all the other tourists but in sober and peaceful solitude reflecting on his future.

Maybe he was inspired by Oscar Wilde's *Discord is to be in harmony with others, to be good is to be in harmony with oneself.*

So at the end of his last day of rafting, instead of climbing into a jeep and heading back to the raft base in the poor heart of the country, he hitched a ride with all the raft crews on the tourists' bus and headed down to the coast.

Ricky and Steve-O got on the bus behind him.

"What's this lads?"

"No worries, Scrambles, we cleared it with the boss, we got ourselves a couple of days off too and figured we'd join the party."

They quickly made friends with the driver, Franklyn, and at the first gas station he agreed to pull over so they could dive in for some rum, coke and a bag of ice.

Franklyn was in a chatty mood and he liked eye contact,

which is polite of course, but maybe not when you are driving forty passengers on a steep and winding mountain road. At night.

Franklyn guessed when it was time to look back at the road by the facial expressions of the passengers in the front seats. Ed lit up a cigarette, but something was wrong. Oh. Yeah. He was already smoking one. The road was straight for a few hundred yards. Franklyn swivelled in his seat.

"So Ed-Ward, are you married in Wales?"

"No, Franklyn, I'm not."

"And do you have wives anywhere else?" Franklyn laughed a big hearty laugh. He laughed a lot, and loud, and guzzled their coke, until the only way they could dilute the rum was with the ice-cubes. It was a warm evening but the ice-cubes were not melting fast enough. This bus was starting to feel like a ship at sea. In a storm. With a mad pirate at the helm.

"Do you know a place to stay?" Ed asked Ricky.

"Sure."

"Is it a B&B? Or a hostel?"

"We are staying where we are staying that is all I can tell you about where we are staying."

At ten the next morning Steve-O and Ed were groggy but hungry. Ricky didn't do mornings so they woke him up, told him it was lunchtime already and went for breakfast at the Cabarete Beach Hotel. Sitting on a rooftop terrace overlooking the azure ocean, with the onshore breeze moving the tablecloth, an all-you-can-eat buffet, a chef to cook your omelette just how you like it and a waiter to top up your coffee. For $4. That's enough to postpone any hangover.

A man with silver hair but much too healthy looking to be described as elderly stood at the top of the steps looking over the tables at the view. He was strong; not the semi-toned bulk that most men of that age call fitness, but lean and light and powerful.

He attracted attention, not because he was loud or wearing outlandish fashion or exclusive labels. There was no gold watch, or bracelets, medallions or oversized rings. His shorts and vest were faded by the sun yet he stood out like a star in daylight.

He had presence. He knew something. The secret.

Something told Ed if he went over there and introduced himself his life would be different. But he didn't.

"Power Hour? What do they mean?"

Ed looked at a chalk board hanging near the bar and checked his watch.

"It means that until eight o'clock if we buy one cuba libre, we get three."

"But that is two?"

"What?"

"Eight o'clock is in two hours. Don't they mean Power *Hours*?"

"Ricky! Don't quibble about the small print, especially when it works in your favour."

Ricky sighed. "I was looking forward to a cold beer. Still I suppose we should go with the flow."

They picked a table on the edge of the sand and an hour later they were well downstream. At five minutes to eight o'clock the boys pushed three tables together so they had somewhere to put the last round of drinks.

"What are they calling the other town where The Travel Rep Girls told us we shouldn't go with our rental mopeds?" Steve-O had two slits for eyes, he looked like an alien.

"Sosua," replied Ed at the third attempt.

"Will we be going on the mopeds to Sosua now?"

Ricky's eyes widened at the thought. A second smiling alien.

The lads moon-walked over to where they had parked the mopeds.

Steve-O's moped had a flat tyre. Ricky revved his engine, Steve-O leapt on the back and they tore off down the street.

Ed had lost his moped key. It was in the secret little built-in pocket in his designer board shorts. He couldn't find the pocket. It was somewhere in those shorts but it was so secret and so little and so well built in. He patted himself front and back, fished and felt and wriggled, then he had an idea.

Standing under a street lamp so he could see properly, he took them off to have a proper look. Coins spilled onto the pavement. Here it is! He went back to the line of mopeds. He was sure his was red. There were four red ones. His key fitted a blue moped on the end of the line.

A moped came blaring back up the road. Steve-O was standing on the seat behind Ricky. Steve-O's left hand gripped Ricky's pony tail, jerking Ricky's head back so he was seeing more stars than road. The front wheel was barely on the ground.

"Eggggg! It's this way – follow us!" wailed Steve-O, his right hand waving theatrically in the air.

The Travel Rep Girls had told them not to bring their mopeds to Sosua because it was a dangerous road. *Ordinarily* it was dangerous because there were no street lights, the road was seriously potholed, cows grazed verges and drunk locals who were as black as the night would be walking home or hitching rides or throwing themselves in front of tourist vehicles for the insurance money. This night it would be *extraordinarily* dangerous because there was no moon.

Tears streamed down Ed's face as he accelerated into the salt wind. When Ricky saw Ed's headlight approaching he started swerving to stop him overtaking. Again as Ed tried to overtake,

Ricky swerved from side to side to block his path. Ed needed a plan.

He dropped back a hundred yards, hunkered down behind the handlebars, tucked his knees into streamlined position and twisted back the throttle. And turned off his headlight.

Ricky and Steve-O both jumped when Ed screamed passed them with millimetres to spare.

The destination was The Triangle which was formed by three infamous night clubs and the numerous bars and cafés in between, all of them open 24/7.

When they arrived they were buzzing, talking and laughing and hopping from one foot to the other so The Travel Rep Girls were a little overwhelmed, but it was clear what had happened; they were caked in dust, with bugs in their hair, stubble and smudged across their t-shirts.

Travel Reps are used to having their advice ignored and being responsible for the consequences. So gallantly, as they walked down the street to the next bar, The Girls offered some more guidance: "Many of the people in this area at this time of night are whores – they come in all ages and both sexes."

"Yep…'kay, 'kay, 'kay got it. Lets go in here…" The boys ducked into a night club. The girls stood on the pavement unbelieving.

There were no windows and the walls were black. There were no lights except for a few over the dance floor and a single bulb over the bar which was a hatch. You could buy rum. Just rum. By the bottle. The boys got coke and ice to go with it.

Suddenly there was a face in their faces. A huge person, probably a man. The whites of his eyes shone like headlights. He flashed a smile.

"Which one of you wants to dance with my girlfriend?"

"What time is it?"

With his right hand Ed lifted up his left wrist so it was in front of their faces. He pushed the light button on his watch so they could read the time. They stared at the watch. Ed pushed another button. The light came on.

"It's four o'fuckin clock."

"What night is this?"

"Tuesday."

"Oh good."

"No, not good, it *was* Tuesday night, now is the morning of today which is Wednesday."

"But we have to be working on Wednesday don't we? Oh baaad."

Ricky and Steve-O were plastered and a thirty-minute moped-death-ride away from two hours sleep followed by a three hour bus-trip to a full day of work.

Ed was retired. A few hours sleep is no problem when you've nothing to do all day. He would have breakfast at the Cabarete Beach Hotel, then maybe walk back along the beach and take a nap.

The owner of the guest house stopped Ed when he arrived back from breakfast. This was probably to do with the missing moped. No. It was about a lady who had just checked in. Guest House Man was pointing at the kitchen door, she was in there. Avoid her, she will talk you to death.

Mmmm. Ed was buzzing on the all-the-coffee-he-could-drink, and floating on the freedom of nothing-to-do-all-day. Avoiding her for a few days could be difficult and spoil his vacation. He decided to go to the kitchen for a chat.

He stood an inch or two inside Talking Lady's safe-space and spoke in an impassioned way about whatever came into his head, in half-finished sentences, barely pausing for breath. In less than a minute her eyes glazed, she had already stepped behind the table to protect herself. Talking Lady made her excuses and left.

That evening Ed was walking on the sand, feeling the grains working under his feet, hearing the sounds of curling water. In a few days he would be flying home to start the next chapter of his life which, he had decided, would be different. Suddenly, and out of nowhere, a lady appeared at his side. She was the colour of sand and only four feet tall. Stone Woman was from Canada and lived on the beach.

"Stones are good for your mind…they keep you healthy… people don't believe that I am forty…do you want to see my amber collection?"

This woman had been washed up on the shore like one of her stones. But no-one wanted to collect her. She so obviously needed a friend, which made her unfriendly.

Guest House Man had offered Ed the use of his long-board. Ed went surfing every day, surfing in shorts in mid-December – that's what he wrote on the post-cards – but it was only half the story.

In his current mood surfing was like drinking sea water. Every great wave hinted at a better one, and a better one again, until the evening when he sat on the sand, exhausted and sunburned, and with salty nuts.

Imagine if there was a way to experience the thrill of riding a wave while sitting peacefully in the shade.

The next day he was sitting in a pressurised cabin watching that little aeroplane symbol inch across the screen towards Europe.

And a few year's later, one early morning on the western edge of Western Europe Ed was watching seagulls in the stream, dipping and thrashing and flapping themselves clean, preparing for another busy day of parading around the rubbish bins in the village and squawking at things.

That evening he watched those same birds; their imperial flight at the cliff-edge.

Which is when it happened. As if he was flying.

behind

They were in the fast lane, the world was standing still.

Ed's head was racing – the thrill of the chase and the fear of crash-and-burn.

The only way to distract himself from the tiny distance between the skin of his knees and the English tarmac was by remembering that his hips were wedged against Henri's behind. His mind revved with lewd images. He tried to remember the fruit of his reflections on desire; that it was insatiable, that even when you get what you want you want more, or different, or both. But that just made it worse!

The only other topic was knees-and-elbows and the tarmac.

Well before they reached the Severn Bridge Ed's nerves were exhausted. He had to give up. Without actually doing it he lifted the visor to let in some fresh air and then, without actually doing it, took off the helmet all together and let the wind blow through his hair.

That's better.

They were in the car park of Morgan's Café. Of all the cafés in all of Wales Henri had brought him to Morgan's. How mad is that!

"That was fun, no? We touched the white and nearly washed

out going through the round-about at Culverhouse Cross, but apart from that…" She was debriefing herself while unzipping her jacket. They were standing by the wall. Or at least she was. Ed was leaning against the wall waiting for the blood to flow back into his legs.

"This was Darren's bike. He called it The Holy Ghost because, he said, if Jesus had ridden a motorbike it would have been this one. When I ride The Ghost I become my brother."

Now she tells me, thought Ed. Sitting behind Dead Darren is a very different ball-game to rear-ending hot Henri.

"It was Darren that got me into bikes originally, when I was fourteen we rode from Cardiff to Betws-y-Coed on the A470. In a car you just get bumped around, but on a bike all the forces balance out and there are some great twisties on that road. There's one, The Fiddler's Elbow at Merthyr, well, we melted into that bend, my heart was pulled down into my body and it changed me forever. I had spots on my face but after that I didn't mind."

Ed was dabbing his feet on the ground testing for feeling, happy to let her talk.

"Riding on that edge between fear and thrill is when I come alive, when I stop seeing one thing after another – that linear mindset dissolves – when I'm on that edge I can see it all, there's no such thing as a blind corner, it's like being on top of the world, with time and space, and none of it in your face.

"For example, cornering at speed, accelerating out of a bend, there is no thinking, just a timeless awareness. That's why I do it – that high – it's addictive. The biggest buzz can leave you feeling the most profound peace."

With that Henri was finished. She seemed satisfied.

Ed was still leaning against the wall but he started writhing with excitement. "Oh no, but yes, exactly. That's it!" He looked into space for a moment. The moment became too long for Henri.

"Are you...?" she prodded.

"I think you've cracked it," Ed said in American accent.

"What have I cracked?"

"The Why. The Why behind extreme and..."

"Are you...?"

"Okay, so, sensation seeking is a booming business, right? Because it's the way for us to hopefully get a taste of The High you just talked about. Of course. Obvious. But what is The High if you unpack it? What's in there? From what you said, and you're right, it's not actually about speed or danger or edge, that's just a means to an end, I'll tell you what it is, except you just told me – *high* is short for *heightened awareness.* The awareness we experience when the present moment blossoms – past and future have been elbowed out of existence – there is only Now. An exquisite Now which contains the trust that you are prepared for anything and everything, an even emotional keel, a felt sense that all the pieces are coming together, or better, realising there are no pieces, that nothing is missing and any sense of self has vaporised. It's all one."

"I was talking about riding..."

"Yes, but it's not about the activity at all at all at all. The thrill is not in the activity – in the adventure or extreme or drug – it's not about the bike – what we are addicted to is *purity of mind!* Which means we don't have to risk our life to feel alive!"

"Oh wo wo, wait a minute, are you sure?"

"Sure I'm sure. I've never been surer. It answers a lot, it answers everything. Because, it's like this, while extreme adventure and meditation appear to be polar opposites – if done right – they both generate, and demand, elevated levels of alertness *and* relaxedness. They both transform the mind in the same way. Which explains why one person, for example me, feels drawn to both. Which means the adrenalin-fuelled, death-defying activity ME, and the recluse-on-a-cliff ME are not in conflict – their motivation and the goal is the same – which is purity of mind. *Are you digging this Henri?* The gift is Heightened Awareness! All the other stuff is just wrapping. "

"I think we need to get a brew down you – with plenty of sugar."

But Ed was on a roll.

"Oh, it gets better. So, we've ascertained that the appeal of all extreme pursuits, and possibly probably maybe most excessive obsessive addictive behaviour, that the appeal of all the above is as a path to Heightened Awareness, okay? So, which way is best? Adrenalin fuelled activity ME? Or the recluse-on-a-cliff ME? Thrill or peace?

"So, well now, recluse-on-a-cliff ME would have to win that one because meditation is not only a path to purity of mind, but also the method to abide by it – to make it last!"

Ed stuck out his tongue Einstein-style, he needed a big blackboard and chalk, he wanted to draw, instead he talked more.

"I have a question for you, Henri. Have you ever found what you are looking for?"

"I've had my moments…"

"Exactly! You have had moments…yes. But *The High* doesn't have to be fleeting and unpredictable, expensive and life-threatening. It is simple – like a pyramid resting on it's base – it's our true way of being! It feels like coming home. To a home we never knew existed. Which is a contradiction I know but don't let that put you off. The feeling is perfect belonging. And that's why it feels so good. It's who *I* really is. That is how *it* really is. It's the meaning and it's the purpose and it's the fulfilment!… Mmmmm…I can smell coffee…and bacon…" Ed was taking his jacket off and putting it on the right way round. "I have spent my whole life preparing and planning, setting up the circumstances to do wild things in faraway places at some time in the future, yet when the pyramid is resting on its base there is nowhere else to be, and nothing else to do."

He stood up straight.

"The adventure is all the time," he said quietly as he looked around, a bit like God did on the seventh day. "Give me a shoulder, will you?"

Ed and Henri walked hip-to-hip towards Morgan's Café.

When the couple entered the café the regulars stopped talking and chewing and sipping. That was Henri. And she had her arms around a guy in an azure blue zoot suit who was mumbling and looked delighted with himself.

As you would.

new flame

The sea has waves days after a storm has passed.

Ed had returned to his cliff top solitude but despite all the insights and resolve he'd generated during the wedding weekend it took him a while to settle.

At first he wasn't sure if he even wanted to – settle that is. It had been fun in the old sense of the word. Now he had withdrawal, see-sawing moods which he addressed with stimulants, and balanced with relaxants, forever over-steering passed the happy medium he was seeking – always busy and nothing to show for it. His head a cauldron of notions.

Years ago he had turned the pages of a coffee-table book of home-made off-the-grid houses: cabins on mountains, lodges in woods, shacks up trees, underground bolt-holes. Remote. Away from troubles and concerns. He had envied these people their peaceful lives. Just looking at these places had brought a sense of relief. Even the memory of it was soothing.

That was years ago. Now Ed had some off-the-grid experience of his own so he knew what was true; sure, some of these nature dwellers enjoyed a peaceful life but only because they were peaceful people.

You don't find Trouble, you bring it with you. Take a polluted mind into a natural world and you will cause environmental disasters.

If it aint inside me, I can't spill it.

His cabin was quiet and simple but if he spent his time generating a list of improvements and complaining about the climate and taking exception to his neighbours (who may live an hour's walk away) he may as well be in a downtown apartment.

It's not about the cabin. *The* idyllic life is here-and-now. Because if he could live happily here-and-now he could live anywhere. The cabin becomes an optional extra.

The wedding weekend had ruffled Ed, and since his return he had hidden in activity, picking up some shifts in the pub, walking Evie Sullivan's dog while she was in hospital, doing his share in the poly-tunnel. He read the book that Tracy had quoted, the Nietzsche, and found a second quote, also about trees, that seemed to fit the moment: *The more the tree wants to rise in the heights and the light, the more determinedly do it's roots strive earthwards…* It was a bit like that for him.

Sure, he had decided that heightened awareness and purity of mind and perfect balance was his lifetime goal and that the surest, best way to arrive there – and remain there – was meditation. And that meditation was free and easy, and could be as simple as sitting on your seat and watching your breath. So how come he resisted it so successfully?

He woke up heavy-headed. The coffee jar was empty, which seemed significant. It was time to make a cut. He walked barefoot across the field to the stream, like he had been doing before the wedding weekend, and dipped his hand in the water and put it on his eyelids and dipped his hand again and put it on the back of the neck. And stood up and felt the wind against his face. That's a good morning!

Gradually he rediscovered simplicity and contentment until, when someone asked him about his "life as a recluse" it came as a surprise, because he had never felt so connected. He felt the texture of tree bark, heard the leaves under his feet and watched the bug crawling to safety. Movement became the meditation. And for weeks that's all he knew. The proverb *Never less alone than when alone* was perfectly true.

Days passed and the clocks changed and it was time to light the stove.

Emptying the ash, cleaning the glass, hauling the logs, crunching the paper, cracking the kindling and, of course, striking the match. The ceremony of it all cheered him as much as the light and heat.

He put a match to the paper and fed it twigs and dried-out hairy ivy roots, laid on some more sticks and shut the door. He sat by the glass and watched the flame as it danced and changed. Living this way there was no black and white, or existent and non-existent – it was all just latent or emergent. He felt the fire's glow on the skin of his face. Which was when there was a knock on the door.

Only once before had there ever been a knock on the door.

She – it was a beautiful, smiling, female face – had short cropped blonde hair, large loop earrings, a leather jacket, long flower dress, and fourteen hole Doc Martin boots with red roses embroidered on them.

"Hello, Ed!"

Henri gave him a hug. He tried to hug her too but the pack on her back made it difficult to get any kind of grip, so it was more of a rub.

Henri was excited. As in agitated. She hopped passed him into the middle of the room, stopping next to the tree trunk that held the roof up.

"Put the kettle on will you? I'm gasping."

Ed had an itchy head. He scratched it. Now Henri was standing in front of the large round window, her eyes fixed by the ocean. "You do have a kettle do you?"

Ed filled the kettle and set it on the stove.

"Well," she said "You're right."

"Right about what?"

"I don't want to die like a bitch in a ditch."

"What?"

"I've packed in my job and given up The Ghost."

"Really?"

"Yep!"

"Why?"

"Because I'm going to be a nun."

"Wow, really!"

"Yep. Either that or I'm going to have babies."

"A nun *or* have babies?...Ookaaay...when will you decide?"

"In the next few minutes."

Acknowledgements

This is a novel, all the bad stuff is myth inspired by the good stuff who are (in no particular order); Mike and Bish, Stu and Rich, Mike and Alison, Lex and Andi, Toneth, Klara, Brian, Alphonse and many others including all the boyz n girlz of nineties Tyrol and noughties Wales. To all the people who owned the sofas we slept on, tables we ate at, boats we floated, cars we cruised in and bars we drank at – Thank You.

Invaluable inspiration was provided by the life and writing of Edward Abbey. I share his heartbreak for a disappearing wilderness and marvel at the humour with which he recorded it. My aspiration is to write, with his skill, on the potential of human being.

Aside from everything by Mr Abbey, significant references for *transpose* would include the ubiquitous *The Tibetan Book of Living and Dying* by Sogyal Rinpoche (Rider, 2008). Also *Into The Wild* by Jon Krakauer (Pan Books, 1998), *Everett Reuss: A Vagabond for Beauty* by W.L. Rusho (Gibbs Smith, 1983) and *Surfing the Edge of Chaos: The Laws of Nature and the New Laws of Business* by Richard T Pascale (Crown Business, 2001). I watched *Fight Club* (Dir. David Fincher, 1999) between each draft.

Thanks to Andrea, Lauryn and my family for giving me a large field to graze in, to Phil for getting up early to read my thoughts, and to Mother Mary and The Angel Sophia for your counsel and correction.

To Orlagh at *Designs for Wellbeing,* thanks for proving it wasn't luck the first time and making our conversation into this cover.

And to Maurice for being the friend and guide to bring *transpose* over the finish line.

Finally, dear Rinpoche, thank you again for giving me my life back.

Matt Padwick, Beara, February 2017

Lightning Source UK Ltd.
Milton Keynes UK
UKOW03f0311040417
298287UK00002B/38/P

9 780993 184031